Whenever You Call

Whenever You Call

Stories of God Delivering Through Hurt, Pain and Struggle

Aurora Avendor

Published by Game Changer Publishing

ISBN 978-1-7365491-7-9

www.PublishABestSellingBook.com

DEDICATION

To my husband, who struggled many nights with disturbed slumber because I needed the lights on to complete one, two, or three more chapters. Thank you for your patience. I love you!

To Fred, for many unrequited kindnesses, including Aurora.

But most of all, this book is dedicated to God Almighty for blessing me with clarity of thought and the inspiration to fulfill my life's dream through Him.

DOWNLOAD YOUR FREE GIFTS

Read This First

Just to say thanks for buying and reading my book, I would like to give you a 100% bonus gift for FREE, no strings attached!

To Download Now, Visit:
www.AuroraAvendorSpeaks.com/freegift

Whenever You Call

Stories of God Delivering Through
Hurt, Pain and Struggle

Aurora Avendor

www.PublishABestSellingBook.com

Foreword

Every now-and-then we come across a literary piece that makes us do a double-take or sit-up and take notice. Maybe it's something that we want to commit to memory. Or perhaps, it's just that good, and we want to reread it over-and-over again.

Aurora Avendor has given us that in her new book *Whenever You Call*. She is so enterprisingly transparent in her story-telling that one has to ask, "Are the stories true?" The book is poignant, heartfelt and written with such depth that you feel like each story is happening to you. Every narrative expresses a realism that can only be told by one who has gone through life's struggles and survived.

Each time that I've read the book, and I read it twice; I hoped to find another short story that wasn't there before. Maybe I had missed one. But to my disappointment, I had not.

Whenever You Call is an uplifting book that you'll want to tell others about; because just as God was there for those who called on him, he'll be there for you too.

I love it, Aurora! See you on the bestseller list.

Victoria Ebenshade

Table of Contents

Introduction

Each day life presents situations that make us question ourselves, others, God, and sometimes life itself. We ask why is this happening to me? What did I do to deserve this? How did I even get here? Especially when our problems seem hopeless, and we want them to just go away! And if possible, remove us as well.

As I wrote this book, I asked myself, *who'll buy it? And why?* Do I know enough about relationships, God, heart-wrenching, or life-altering situations to keep someone interested in reading about them while providing insight and encouragement? And then I answered. *Yes. I do!*

When it comes to life, one doesn't want to hear from an ingenue or someone inexperienced about the facts of life, but rather someone who has tasted life's bitter fruit and rode its ups and downs. I have eaten the fruit and taken the ride, and yet, I remain.

This book was written for adults by an adult. It talks about adult situations, like marriage, infidelity, friendship, and disappointment. Some stories should make you laugh – others should make you think. But all should turn you towards God's listening ear.

Life holds no guarantees. We lose those we love, and if we live long enough, the pain of life is inevitable. We will never understand the ways of God or why life happens as it does, and that's a fact! But life goes on.

God never promised that our life would be free from the travail that accompanies it. He never said that lessons-learned would be easy; because they aren't. But what He does promise – is to be there *whenever you call*. And God is not man that he should lie. So hold Him to His word.

CHAPTER 1

An Angel in the Spring

The word Angel has many definitions:

~ Typically, benevolent celestial being that acts as an intermediary between heaven and earth.

~ A messenger of God; a supernatural being, either good or bad, attributed greater than human power.

~ Spiritual being attendant upon God.

~ A guardian spirit or guiding influence.

Those are all good, but my definition is—***The one who saved my life.***

It was a beautiful spring morning with birds chirping, the sun shining, breezes blowing, clear skies, and me driving in my new car. I couldn't ask for a more perfect day. As I went to work, I engaged in my usual *driving-to-work practices.* You know, listening to my favorite Christian station, sipping a Vanilla Cappuccino, and intermittently applying make-up at streetlights and stop signs, a wonderful day, right? Wrong! Something was going on! I couldn't put my finger on it, but I had an uneasy feeling that someone was watching me. Not only that, but I thought I had seen an **angel** in the sky. That's right, an angel!

I didn't see a halo. Nor did I hear a musical arrangement of harps, trumpets, symbols, lyres, or other musical instruments that TV perpetuates when one has this type of sighting. No, I didn't get a little cupid fluttering through the sky either. But I did see something! And whatever it was, it was sent by God to protect me personally. It wasn't something tangible that I could touch, but more like a silhouette that I could see as it hovered in front of and behind my car, peering at me through the clouds. It had enormous, pallid wings, each the size of several large mansions if you can imagine that, with a massive body like a thousand clouds, rolled into one. I couldn't see its eyes because the radiance of its smile almost blinded me. Oh yes, it was smiling, smiling at me. As the sun beamed through its silhouette, I saw every color of the rainbow. I was mesmerized.

HONK! HONK!

The deafening horn of the Mercedes behind me emphatically stated that I was holding up traffic. I tried to get another glimpse but couldn't. When I looked again, the angel was gone. *Angels???* I thought… *you need to get a grip.* Were the clouds playing tricks on me?

I was listening to Rev. Dr. Louise Williams on the radio. She had just finished playing a song by the Norwood Sisters, and now she was beginning to pray. As usual, I began praying with her.

I don't know from where or how it came, but suddenly I was overwhelmed with a feeling that I couldn't shake. It was so strong that it stopped me from praying. Was it fear... dread... shame... sorrow? I didn't know. Only one word could describe it, OVERWHELMING! The feeling compelled me to cry and talk out loud to God. I couldn't stop! I began praying the same prayer over and over and over. *"Forgive me, God, for all that I've done. Bless my family and me, and to let your angels protect us throughout the day."* The tears fell so fast that they blurred my vision. I wanted to pull the car over but continued driving because I knew God was protecting me despite my tears. Then just like that, I could no longer pray. It was as if someone had bridled my tongue. I couldn't speak; I wanted to, but words wouldn't come out. I could only cry and groan. The only word I could utter was JESUS. But in my mind, I kept saying, *"Father, forgive me. Father, protect my family and me. Let your angels stand guard around us."*

Fifteen minutes later, I was almost back to normal. Just as quickly as the feeling came... it left. But something was different; I felt purged, clean, refreshed, and uplifted. It was the strangest thing.

What the heck was that? I wondered. Either I was getting a message from God, or... it was time for Prozac!! *Where's my water?* ☺

* * * * * * * * * *

I arrived at work, ready to start my day. Still overwhelmed by the car experience, I'd almost forgotten that it was Wednesday, payday, shopping day; in short, Debbie's day. I strategically mapped out my stores. After all, I only had an hour (ha, ha). Since our checks came in the morning, by 10:30, I was ready to go. Wednesdays were my "early lunch to avoid the crowd days." I looked forward to them. I still felt a little strange, but shopping was my panacea for all ills and should not be ruined because I had an encounter of the third kind. So, like a good soldier, I shook it off.

11:45. I said to myself. I'm *late, and I still have to stop at the bank to deposit my check.*

That's when I saw Billy, an old friend, whom I hadn't seen in years, walking towards me.

"Hey, Billy."

"Hel...Hel...Hello, Debbie."

Not mocking him, but Billy had a terrible stutter. Usually, it took him about five minutes to finish the first word, let alone the sentence.

We performed the customary old friend embrace, chatted for a few minutes, and tried to catch up, but it was getting late. Ten minutes later, he was still yapping, and I had banking to do.

"I've gotta go, Billy. I'm in a hurry. Call me."

What a talker, I thought, as I entered the bank.

I opened the glass doors and smiled. The bank was empty. I was the only customer. *Good, I'll get right in-and-out. No long lines today.* I walked up to the counter, placed my bags on the floor, and pulled out my check. After the usual formalities (showing the ID, signing the check, etc.), I waited for my cash. After counting it, I realized I hadn't deposited any (a girl's gotta cover her checks). I was writing out my deposit slip - when from nowhere - a man's hand covered my money and grabbed it from the counter. Naturally, I thought it was my friend, Billy, playing games. As I turned to face him, my smile faded, and my heart sunk. It wasn't Billy at all, but a rather tall, lanky, bald man, whom I didn't know. He had snatched my money and was running out of the bank.

"Stop, thief!" I screamed. "Help, I'm being robbed!"

Bank employees scurried to their feet at the commotion. As the nervous stranger tried to exit the bank, I hesitantly, unthinkingly pursued him. I didn't think about my life or that he may have had a gun. I only saw my money bouncing as he ran away with my salary. By the time I reached him, he had flung open the door and was darting across the street and through the park.

"Stop, thief! Stop!"

A police officer sitting in his van heard me screaming as I exited the bank. I ran towards him breathlessly, trying to explain what happened.

"He... he..." (trying to catch my breath). "That man... heeee... he stole my money!"

"Go back into the bank, Miss," he said, as he radioed for assistance, then took off running after the robber.

The bank was buzzing with excitement when I returned. Bank employees were huddled in clusters discussing what happened. Newly appeared customers were covering their mouths, looking at me in shock. Making my way through the sea of whispers and the "are you all rights." Joan, the bank president's assistant, led me to his office with a print-out in one hand and a cup of coffee for me in the other. Marva, a teller, walked in tow, bringing my purse and packages with her. It was then that I realized how shaken I was. The president talked for twenty minutes, but I never heard a word.

Forty minutes later, the policeman returned to the bank with what looked like the whole police force.

"Did you catch him?" I asked excitedly. His eyes answered before he did.

"No. He got away, but we have his description."

"His description!" I repeated, "What does that mean? What about my money? Suppose you don't catch him, then what?"

"I don't know, Miss. We'll do our best. Let's get started on your statement."

Several employees and I began to explain what happened. We watched as officer Benton conscientiously wrote down every word, scratching-out here, highlighting there, confirming this, repeating that. Questions. Questions. Questions. When he finally finished his report, he pulled me aside.

"Do you know how blessed you are, young lady?" He said, "You must have an angel watching over you."

"Blessed!!!" I screeched. "How do you figure that? "The man robbed me! He stole a week's pay. Plus, he could have killed me! That doesn't sound like a blessing to me!"

"You're right," he repeated, "he could have killed you – but he didn't. He stole your money – not your life. He probably had all intentions of robbing the bank at gunpoint but saw your money on the counter and decided the money was a better risk. That money probably saved everyone's life."

That's when it hit me, the car, the crying, the praying, the Angel; God was letting me know that something was about to happen. But through it all, He protected me. Remember my prayer, "Let your angels protect us." In His magnificent way, He forewarned me. He didn't stop it, but He pulled me through. Not only that, but He showed me Divine favor as well. The bank manager credited my account with the entire stolen amount, gave me free checking for my account's life, and a $1,500 prepaid visa card to spend a day relaxing (Translation–another Debbie Day).

I beamed with happiness as I walked back to work because God had spared my life, returned my money, showed me favor, and allowed me to find the perfect sales during my shopping spree. Isn't God wonderful!?

He manifested himself through my tears and gave an angel the job of protecting me, and it did! Even with today's high rate of unemployment and a crumbling economy, Angel still has a job.

CHAPTER 2

She Opened the Door, and His Lies Walked In

"Do you Esmeralda take Thaddeus to be your lawfully wedded husband? To have and to hold, for better or worse, for richer or poorer, till death, do you part?"

"I do."

"And do you Thaddeus take Esmeralda to be your lawfully wedded wife? To have and to hold, for better or worse, for richer or poorer, till death, do you part?"

"I do."

※ ※ ※ ※ ※

In retrospect, Essie could honestly say that Thad's wedding vows to her were the biggest lies she had ever heard. Fourteen months had passed since then, and to date, he hadn't kept one promise.

Essie Valentine prepared to enjoy the marriage of a lifetime, her second one, her final one. What she thought would last forever had disappointingly exhausted itself in less than two years. Instead of happy trails, her fourteen months of marriage were co-equaled by fourteen months of separation. Regrettably, happiness was nowhere in sight.

"I know you'd never get married again, Essie, would you?"

"Why wouldn't I?" she questioned with sincere honesty.

"Essie, you've got to be kidding me," said a surprised Violet, almost choking on her sandwich. "Look at the way he did you. I would never want to get married again if I were you. I couldn't take the pain."

"Why, Vie, because it didn't work out?"

"No, Essie, because Thad was a bum, a bum who broke your heart and bounced from woman to woman while married to you. You cared for his children; you took care of him. In addition to that, you found him two jobs after he lost his. And what did he do? He dumped you because he didn't want the responsibility of being a married man. In less than two years, he left you with no money, no car, and no home. He left you to fend for yourself, never once asking if he could help you in any way. Thank God that you're a go-getter, and you were able to bounce back because he left you with NOTHING, Essie. Except 'A BROKEN HEART'! That's why I'd never get married again. You're a much stronger woman than you think. I would have crumbled."

"She's right, Essie," interjected Lyla, the only happily married one of the group. "I hate to talk about your husband, but as Vie said, he was a real dog. You two had just returned from vacation, and he secretly started the process of dumping you. You're thinking about eternity. He's thinking escape! What kind of stuff is that? The ink hadn't dried on your marriage license, and fourteen months later, he's gone. I don't know what I'd do if Carl did something like that to me?"

"Are you kidding? With your temper, you'd give him your size tens until he choked on the shoelaces. That's what you'd do," laughed Essie, pointing towards Lyla's plaid Gucci sneakers with black laces.

Vie and Lyla had been her best friends for as long as she could remember, and this was their Saturday night! The night they laughed, cried, discussed, planned, and were as brutally honest as their friendship would allow, which in most cases was pretty straightforward. This was the night they could be themselves and discuss all the hurt, happiness, joy, sadness, anger, and any other emotions they felt about husbands, work, children, boyfriends, or whatever. In short, this was "Girls Night." Theirs was a combination of *Girlfriends* meets *Living Single* meets *Sex in the City*. But instead of taking place in the studio, it took place in Essie's home once a month on a Saturday Night.

Tonight, all conversation centered on Essie. Tonight, she was the bird with the broken wing, and it was her turn to lovingly accept the counsel, which she had, so often, and tenderly rendered. Her mood grew somber. "You both know that I'll get through this, don't you?

And you're right; I'm hurting. I don't know if it's because he didn't love me or that he left me for another woman. That hurts so bad."

"Or…." Lyla began.

"Or what, Lyla? Go ahead, say it."

"Truthfully, Essie, maybe it's because you realize what a horrible mistake you made by divorcing Sonny. Sure, he had control issues, but he did love you, girl, and you loved him. Maybe he was demanding and sometimes mean as hell, but you two made such a cute couple, and he was willing to get counseling. But let's face it; once Thaddeus hit the scene, all bets were off with Sonny."

Essie's head hung towards the floor. Somehow for her, Girls Night had lost its flavor. "I know you both love me," she said, trying not to cry, "but it's time for me to love myself."

"You know we're here for you, girl," they both said in unison as they rallied together for a group hug.

"I'm tired, ladies, and I've got church in the morning. We'll talk later in the week." After good nights all around, she straightened up, discarded the leftovers, and prepared for a much-needed rest. "Why?" she asked herself just before falling to sleep.

Sometimes the truth hurts

* * * * * *

Her eyes weren't fully opened the next morning before the question, *why did I do it?* popped into her head. The sun was shining, but drawn bedroom curtains provided a welcomed comfort of darkness. She needed darkness. It was an excellent place to hide sadness and pain. She wanted to kick herself for being so stupid and ignoring every inner feeling. She always prided herself on doing the right thing, the smart thing, but not this time. This time she had been as foolish as they come. And now… now, she felt sad… unhappy… alone. Still, she had to face it. Her marriage was over, and from the looks of it, Thad wasn't coming back. Did she want him back?

Why couldn't this have happened to me in my twenties? She asked herself. *Why, at forty-three years old, did I leave the man I adored for someone who didn't love me?* She could feel the tears coming. *No need feeling sorry for myself now*, she thought, reaching for a Kleenex. But she did feel sorry for herself, and no amount of tissue could wipe away her tears. They were far too many.

She stopped reminiscing and switched off her alarm clock. The annoying sound could wake the dead. It was after nine a.m. Her brother would soon pick her up for church, something she rarely missed on Sunday mornings, no matter how tired she was. Pulling herself from the bed, she walked towards the bathroom but turned to answer her ringing phone. She smiled, hearing her brother's voice on the other end of the line.

"Hi, Mel. No, I'm not ready yet. How long before you get here? I'll be ready. See you then."

She jumped in and out of the shower before the hot running water turned cold. Five to ten minutes of hot water was all it would produce at one time. Experience had taught her to wash the essential areas first and then jump out. It was definitely time for a new water heater. What to wear? She asked the same question of herself every Sunday. After 15 minutes of personal grooming and 10 minutes of dressing, she could hear Melvin's horn beckoning her. She darted out the door to his awaiting vehicle and his hearty "hello."

Melvin looked at his watch. "I can't believe it! You're never on time, Essie. What happened today?"

She smiled, looking past him to his wife. "Good morning, Elaine. I'm not listening to your husband. He's just trying to give me grief."

"Pay him no mind, Essie. He's been rushing me all morning."

"Don't worry, Elaine, I'm not."

For a few minutes, the ride was quiet. Essie hoped that her brother would not ask the dreaded question, but as usual, he did.

"Did you hear from him, Essie? Did Thad call you?"

"No, Mel, he didn't."

"I don't know why you ever married him. I told you from the beginning that he was no good. Maybe Sonny wasn't the greatest, but he loved you and was willing to change. I know it wasn't your fault entirely. People tend to think illogically when it comes to matters of the heart. And you're no different, but Essie, why did you marry a bum like Thad?" She wished she could have answered his question, but she couldn't.

Although marriage to her first husband, Sonny, wasn't perfect, she regretted leaving him and wished she had been stronger and more determined to make their marriage work. She acknowledged the fact that no matter how many times Sonny scolded, nagged, criticized, or wielded his tongue like a curette, scooping out self-esteem, it was she who had stepped outside of their marriage. At times, she wished they could have reconciled but knowing him as she did, she felt he would never trust her again. Hers was the ultimate betrayal. Now she was experiencing the ultimate retribution. Was her infidelity coming to exact its revenge through Thad? She didn't know, but she knew these thoughts were too heavy and too depressing for Sunday morning. Still, she wondered if the adage *what goes around - comes around* was correct. Was she receiving her payment through pain? She dismissed the heaviness of the hour, closed her eyes, and attempted to enjoy the ride to church.

God Can Heal All Things

* * * * *

Mondays at Essie's Eatery were mentally exhausting. There were always too many customers with too many emotional hurts from the weekend. On that day, her job description would change from cafe owner to that of counselor, psychiatrist, spiritual advisor, friend, mother, or relationship therapist, providing whatever emotional panacea her patients needed to get them through the day or night. Her customers loved her. She knew how to make each of them feel special; aside from that, the food was delicious.

She milled around the cafe turning on lights, ovens, small appliances, and whatever else was needed to ready her for the day. Most mornings, she'd arrive at 5:00 a.m. and open up. Dexter, her short-order cook, would meet her at 5:15. His was a routine of chopping, dicing, boiling, thawing, browning, stirring, frying, and whatever else was needed to prepare him for 6:00 a.m. breakfast orders, and he was always on time. He was a fantastic cook with a pleasant temperament and corny jokes, which he'd deliver throughout the day. But all-in-all, he was wonderful, and she felt blessed to have him. She had worked hard to open her own business, and it was great if you didn't consider that she rose six days a week before sunrise and often stayed long after it set. Maybe her café wasn't famous like Spago, but it was hers, all hers. She had opened it with her first husband, Sonny, long before she'd ever met Thad. After her divorce from Sonny, she struggled for more than a year to keep it going until finally, it paid off. She was even able to purchase a beautiful condominium after her break-up with Thad. God was good to her. She thought she'd sink after each marital collapse, but she never did because He kept her afloat.

Funny, she thought, *her marriage with Sonny broke up because she **felt** alone, and now that her marriage with Thad was over, she **was** alone.*

She sat behind the counter, thumbing through the morning paper. Thank God, the morning rush was over. Before she knew it, lunchtime had come and gone. It was almost 3 o'clock; she could finally get to her paperwork. She could hear Benny, her dishwasher, rattling pots and pans and muttering to Dexter about being a little neater when he cooked. As usual, Dexter good-naturedly told him to "shut up" and get ready to wash the next stack of things coming his way.

The counter phone rang just before 4:00 p.m. It was Violet's name on the caller ID.

"Hi, Vie."

"Hey, Essie. Are you getting ready to leave?"

"No, girl. I'll be here for another hour or so. I'm getting ready to work on a supply order. What's up?"

"You'll never guess who I saw today."

"Who?"

"Take one guess."

"I don't know, Vie, Who?"

"Sonny!"

"Sonny?!" Shrieked Essie.

"Yea… girl, Sonny!"

"Where did you see him at?"

"At the market on 5th Street. I was at the deli counter when he walked up and said, 'Hello.'"

Essie switched the phone to her other ear, "At the deli counter? It figures Sonny always did like lunch meat. Was he alone?"

"He was alone and asking about you."

"About me?"

"Yep. How is Essie doing? When was the last time I saw you? Is Essie doing this? Is Essie doing that? He even asked, how's the dog? He still loves you, Essie. He said he missed you and that the divorce was his entire fault. He said he didn't blame you for leaving him."

Essie switched ears again, "You guys talked about all that at the deli counter?"

"Yes, we did, but it was mostly him. He knew that I'd tell you. That's why he poured his heart out. And guess what?"

"What?"

"He made it clear that he is still single and asked if I thought that you and Thad would get back together."

"What did you say, Violet?"

"What could I say, Essie, but the truth?"

"And what was that?"

I said, "I hope not."

"Violet!!"

"Well, Essie, it's true. Maybe you and your first husband could get back together if you divorce that Thaddeus! Let's face it; he was never marriage material. But that was your man, and you know my mantra *if you like him - I love him!*"

"Yeah, right! Goodbye Violet. I'll call you later."

"Bye, Essie. Love you."

"Love you back."

Essie returned to her seat at the counter. *Sonny*, she thought, *he almost had it all; business savvy, a degree in molecular physics, body solid as a rock, and boy, could he lay the pipe. Big pipe. African pipe.* If being honest, she had to admit that there weren't many men who could out-do Sonny. He was the full package, in-and-out of the sheets. He always kissed her, and if she hugged him, he would always hug her back and hold her tight, real tight. Sometimes he could be so romantic. Essie loved him. He loved her back, but Sonny's love was hard, real hard. Sometimes he could, and would say the most hurtful things. It was his form of control. Aside from that, Sonny was known to sling a hand or two if he felt the need; therein laid the problem, Sonny's problem. Although she adored him, he often treated her like a third-world wife. But she wasn't a third-world wife, and no woman should be treated like one. Accepting Sonny's archaic customs wasn't then and would never be her forte.

Sonny came from poor beginnings, but once in the United States, he excelled in business. Sonny was brilliant in many areas, but his arrogance and brilliance walked side-by-side; until sometimes, he was intolerable, at best. Sonny always found reasons to criticize. His criticisms and the constant reminder that if not for him, she would still be selling phones at the Corner of Broad and Erie forced her to envisage divorce more often than not. Yet when he wanted to be, Sonny Valentine, whose name changed from Oba-Vulentundi, when he became a citizen, was as charming as a man could be. It was hard to believe that the dictator visiting the cafe during the day was the same passionate man she slept with at night. If Chaka Khan was "everywoman," then Sonny Valentine was "everyman," and most of them… were crazy!

A typical phone conversation with Sonny always consisted of what Sonny wanted. What Sonny needed, or what Sonny wanted her to do.

"Are you busy?"

"No, Sonny. I only have a few customers; how are you?"

"Are you coming straight home tonight, Esmeralda?"

"Yes."

"Good…Stop by my office and pick up the paperwork I left on my desk. Then stop by the market and get goat meat and palm oil. Pick up my pants from the cleaners. Then stop by the ATM. Then do this… then do that." His requests always seemed endless.

"Sonny!" She'd snap, "how about saying, please?" Would it kill you to be appreciative sometimes and stop being so demanding?

"Why do I have to say, please? You're my wife. It's your job to do for me. Like I do for you. Do your job, Esmeralda. I'll see you when you get home."

"Bye, Sonny."

"Essie…Essie…"

"What, Sonny?"

"One more thing…"

"What?"

"I brought you that red fox coat that you were admiring. So bring that beautiful body home so that I can make love to my wife while she's in it. That's what. Bye."

That's what made Sonny so hard to leave. Just when she was ready to spew obscenities at him, he'd say or do something to blow her mind, and she'd fall victim every time. After five years of marriage, he still ordered her about like a handmaiden, and she hated it. But talking to him about it was pointless. He'd dismiss her grievances as quickly as she made them.

Sonny loved the way she took care of him. She was his chef, valet, maid, personal assistant, errand girl, physician, private dancer, and at least four times a week, his naked masseuse. That was the role she enjoyed most of all. After his bath, she would dry him off and then rub him down with oil. Her strong hands would massage each part of his body with expert, tender, loving care. He would lie on his stomach, with eyes closed, anxiously awaiting her to start. He loved it, and he loved her. But appreciation in Sonny's world was short-lived. She was the beautiful flower in Sonny's garden, which he often forgot to water.

Some things are hard to forget

* * * * * *

Essie. Essie. I'm leaving for the day. Essie!!!

She stopped daydreaming and turned to see Dexter looking perplexedly at her. "Essie," he said, putting one arm into his jacket, "You must be in some real deep thought. Did you hear a word I said?"

"I'm sorry, Dex. I was thinking about something. What did you say?"

"I said, put in an egg, bread, and cheese order for tomorrow."

"Is that all?"

"Oh," he continued, "…and bacon."

"I thought we had bacon."

"We're almost out."

"Okay," she said with a smile.

"And…," he continued, "Order some coffee and sugar."

"All right."

"….and butter, and navy beans, and tomatoes, and…"

She lifted her head from her paperwork. Dexter, why didn't you make out a list instead of rattling off 100 items. You know I don't like running out of stock."

She could see Benny laughing from the kitchen as Dexter winked at him.

"I'm only kidding, Essie. I don't need anything. See you tomorrow."

"Goodnight, Dexter."

Seconds later, Benny made his departure from the kitchen, ready to leave as well. "See you tomorrow, boss."

"Goodnight, Benny."

"Goodnight."

Essie prepared to leave as well. The mound of paperwork would have to wait until tomorrow; she was tired and only running on fumes. Assisting her server in the morning and crunching numbers in the afternoon had left her exhausted. She just wanted to go home and indulge in a hot bath. If she still had the energy, a light meal would be optional, and finally, some much-needed sleep. By 10:00 p.m., she had luxuriated in the tub for an hour, dined on turkey and cheese on wheat bread, and was now ready to watch the 11 o'clock news. *Better check my voice messages*, she said to herself just before clicking off the bedroom light.

"You have one new message."

Probably a bill collector, she thought as she hit the play button.

"Hello, Essie. Hello. Essie, are you there? It's me, Thad. Pick up. O.K, I'll call you tomorrow."

As her stomach did major flip-flops, she sat straight up in bed. All traces of sleep had vanished. *Was that Thad?* She asked herself. Rewind tape… Listen… rewind tape… listen again… rewind. "Oh my gosh! That was Thad." She wondered what his call meant. He hadn't called her in a long time. If she remembered correctly, the last time she saw him in passing, snow was on the ground.

Fourteen months had passed since their separation; fourteen long months of hurt, anger, frustration, disappointment, and other emotions she dared not let surface. Fourteen months of asking *why did she let him into her life?*

She remembered the first day they met. She should have turned away from his initial glance, but she didn't. Although not particularly handsome, he was charming in an unsophisticated sort of way. She knew he was a ladies' man. It was written all over him. Not too tall, only about 5'10" but rugged, strong, the way one would expect a construction worker to be. His muscles bulged from every area of his chiseled chest, arms, and thighs and even from that area between his legs that a lady should never stare at, at least not in polite company. But she was no lady, and Thaddeus Tisdale was hard not to notice. He wasn't exceptional, but the man oozed sex-appeal. You know the type, rough-rider, putting down serious ghetto love. His brown skin and

26

naughty boyish grin enthralled her... excited her... enticed her. Maybe it was the bandana tied around his head, or maybe the way his skin looked in that yellow jacket, or maybe it was just because he paid her the attention that Sonny should have been paying. Who knew, but whatever it was, Esmeralda Valentine liked it.

"Hi, gorgeous. How are you?" was the first question he posed while standing in line, waiting for her to ring-up his meal and purchases. She was educated, poised, and out of his league. He knew it. He didn't care. She was tall, attractive, and built like two Coca-Cola bottles joined together. She looked the way he liked a woman to look, with full, juicy, suckable lips. The kind he liked to kiss. The ones he would kiss. He never took his eyes off of her. She could feel him looking into the real sadness of her soul. Every instinct told her to ignore him, but she didn't. There was something about the way he looked and spoke that captivated her.

"I'm fine, and you?" She could feel herself blushing, not wanting to succumb to his conversation, but she couldn't help it. He was asking all of the right questions and saying the right things.

"What's your name?" He asked, placing his items on the counter.

She didn't answer.

"Let me start again. My name is Thaddeus, but most people call me Thad. Now your turn, what's your name?" He asked again.

"Essie."

"Essie?" He repeated. "That's an unusual name. Is it short for something?"

"Yes. It's short for Esmeralda."

"ES-MER-ALDA." He said again, slowly emphasizing almost every syllable. "That's a pretty name for a pretty woman. Are you married, Esmeralda?"

"Yes. I am."

That should have been the end of the conversation. But it wasn't. He came by daily to buy something, cigarettes or gum, food or drink. Sometimes he'd wait around until the other customers left so that he could talk with her alone. Each day he'd ask more and more questions, befriending her, listening to her, comforting her, as she divulged more and more about her life until he knew all there was to know about her troubled five-year marriage to Sonny.

She liked Thad. She blushed at the thought of kissing him. After all, she was married, but Sonny was so darn mean sometimes. Maybe if he were kinder, erotic sentiments from another man would have no effect on her. But he wasn't, and they did. Thaddeus knew what her marriage was lacking, and he readied himself to give it to her. At forty-five years old, he knew how to make a woman feel special. He would make her feel special–something she hadn't felt in a long time.

"What's wrong with this picture, Girl? Watch out!" This phrase repeated itself in her mind daily. The problem was, she didn't listen.

Oops! About to make a bad decision

* * * * * *

The ongoing months posed nothing but problems between her and Sonny; each week, new arguments would develop, some big, some small, some valid, some not. Even if she could magically ship his butt back to Africa, he wouldn't go! Her suffering marriage took on the form of dalliances with Thad. He knew it was only a matter of time before Sonny's woman would be his woman. He didn't know Sonny personally and only saw him from time-to-time at the café, but he didn't like him. If asked why he disliked Sonny, Thaddeus could probably give a million unfounded reasons, but the only one that mattered was how he treated Esmeralda. If she gave him the opportunity, Thaddeus would show Sonny how to treat a wife.

After months of am/pm conversations with her, it was time to ask her out. His timing couldn't have been better; especially, since she had just had a big blowout with Sonny. Thad knew she needed a break.

"What time do you get off work tonight, Miss Esmeralda?"

"You know I close at four, and we're usually gone by five. Why?" she inquired. Although having an idea of where his conversation was going, she went along for the ride.

"How about a drink after work? I know a nice little spot in Center City."

She looked at him, saying nothing. For a moment, he thought she was going to say no. To his surprise, she accepted.

"I can leave a little early," she said. "Can we meet around 5:30?" he asked. Is that too early?"

"No. 5:30 is fine. Can you meet me at Gloria's at 24th & Spring Garden?"

"Sure," she responded, "I love jazz. Plus, Gloria has good food. I'll meet you there."

As she readied herself for her meeting with Thad, she could hear God's gentle voice saying, "no. No Esmeralda. You're married." But she didn't want to hear God. She wanted to hear Jazz at Gloria's. And she wanted to hear it with Thaddeus Tisdale.

It was early in the afternoon, and Gloria's was emptier than full. It was small... quaint. Not at all a place that she thought he'd pick. It boasted white linen tablecloths, with candles on each table. It was cozy and dimly lit. It was the perfect spot for a non-sexual but intimate rendezvous. She sat alongside him at the bar.

"May I have dry, Bombay Sapphire martini for the lady and an Absolute on the rocks for me?

"Oh, you remembered what I told you, huh, Thad."

"Yea... I did."

She sipped her martini and admired the beautiful décor. She was impressed. Thad guzzled his first drink. She could tell he was nervous. So was she. If she counted the five years she'd been married to Sonny plus the two years she dated him, she hadn't been out with another man for seven years. But Thad made her feel comfortable. That's what it was; Thad was comfortable.

After finishing her first drink, she began to feel a bit more relaxed. He talked about his life, his kids, and his desire for her. He showered her with compliments, but she could hardly hear them. All she could think about was kissing him.

"How long can you stay out?" he asked, wishing she could say all night but knowing she would not, even if she could.

"I don't know, until around 8:00."

"Good. It's only 5:45. That gives me two-plus hours to learn more about you, Essie."

"Learn more," she repeated. "Like what? I've been talking to you for months."

"Like what makes Esmeralda Valentine tick."

He watched her laugh. He liked seeing her laugh. She was refreshing, different from other women he knew. She was charming and sexy. And very sweet in an unpretentious sort of way. She was like a delicious piece of candy that you wanted to eat slowly and savor each moment before it was gone.

"Thad, why are you staring at me?" She was now on her second drink and feeling quite coquettish.

"Lean closer, and I'll tell you."

She leaned in as he caressed the back of her neck, gently pulling her closer to him. He discreetly let his tongue glide slowly from her jaw, up the side of her face, before it finally rested in the cleft of her ear. He allowed it to linger there for a moment exploring the softness of her ear. The warmth of his breath and the sensuality of his tongue excited her. Her inhibitions were fading. She felt herself becoming non-restraint, dripping with excitement. She closed her eyes and kissed him as if there were no other people in the restaurant.

"Ummm," he said, savoring the sweetness of her lips.

"Right back at ya," she panted breathlessly.

He knew as well as she that it was just a matter of time until their dalliances would cease to exist, and a relationship would begin. Had she known what heartache lay ahead, that would have been their first and last encounter, but she didn't - and it wasn't. Six months later, she had left Sonny and was dating Thad. Within a year, they were married.

Everyone knows you never marry a bad boy

* * * * * * *

"I told you he'd call you, didn't I?" stated Lyla, waiting to hear Essie's confirmation of her psychic prediction.

Lyla, Essie, and Vie were all on a three-way phone conference discussing "The Thaddeus Call," which translated to a CODE RED EMERGENCY, which meant Leave Everyone! And Stop everything!

"What did he say?" asked Vie as she multi-tasked between her phone conversation and surfing the web. As far as she was concerned, Thad could go to hell and take his code red, code blue, or whatever phone conversation with him. To her, he wasn't worth the time of day, especially after the way he had treated her friend. But whether she liked him or not, she would always be there for Essie, even if it meant listening to her at 1:00 in the morning.

"He said he'd call me tomorrow."

"Essie," said Lyla, "Play the message for us. Let me hear his tone. You know I'm Psychic, girl."

Vie burst into laughter after Lyla's forceful declaration of being able to deal with the paranormal.

Rewind tape… Listen… rewind tape… listen again… rewind. Essie played the tape three times; that was two times too many. They all knew he was up to no good, and you didn't have to be psychic to figure that out.

"Essie, be honest," said Lyla, "Do you really want him back?"

"No. I don't think so, but I'm willing to hear what he has to say."

"Well, when you talk to him, remember these words," said Lyla yawning in between them:

"Neither a borrower nor a lender be.
For loan oft loses both itself and friend,
And borrowing dulls the edge of husbandry.
This above all, to thine own self, be true,
And it must follow, as the night the day,
Thou canst not then be false to any man,
Farewell; my blessing season this in thee."

After Lyla disconnected, Essie and Vie both agreed that even if their friend wasn't psychic, she was sure enough crazy! Who in their right mind would recite Act I, Scene 3 of Hamlet, during a CODE RED EMERGENCY phone call?

A *friend in need – is a friend indeed*

✻ ✻ ✻ ✻ ✻

Ahhh, Wednesday, thought Essie, rolling from one side of the bed to the other. On Wednesdays, Dexter would open the café, giving her a break from her early morning schedule. She could sleep until 9:00 a.m. if she wanted to, and be in by 10:00–a benefit of employing competent staff.

Her phone rang just before 7:45. "Hello."

"Hi. Essie"

Realizing who it was, she dropped the phone.

"Essie? Are you there?"

Nervously… "Yes. I'm here. Hello Thad? How are you?"

"I'm Fine. Did I wake you?"

"No, I was just resting before getting up for work."

"Essie, I'd like to talk with you today. Can I meet you after work?"

She could feel her innards trembling. After a deep breath for composure, she answered. "Yes. What's going on?" She asked, awaiting his response.

"I'd like to talk to you about a few things. Is that OK?"

"OK," she responded.

"Good. Is 8:00 tonight, ok? Will you be home by then? Fine. I'll come over around 8:00. I'll see you then, Essie."

Although she'd seen him in passing once or twice, this would be their first meeting since the separation. She had tried to call him on several occasions, but he either quickly eschewed her calls or only provided minimal conversation. Thaddeus had made it painfully evident that he wanted no bother. And though he never said it, she knew that part of the reason was guilt. *Why now?* She wondered. *What does he want?*

She wanted to call her brother to update him but declined just in case Thad didn't show. She'd gone through that embarrassment before. No more looking foolish for her. After a lunch hour visit to the beauty shop, she left work early and went home.

8:00, 8:27, 8:45, no Thad. *He's up to his old tricks again,* she thought, as she grabbed her remote control and flipped through the channels. Grey's Anatomy was about to start at 9:00 p.m. when the doorbell rang. She took a deep breath, opened it, and smiled. "Hello, Thad." Her heart pounded as she faced the man who broke her heart.

"Hi, Essie. Sorry, I'm late."

What else is new, she thought to herself, eyeing him quickly as he stepped inside. He'd lost a little weight and needed a haircut, but overall he still looked the same. His smile warmed her. His embrace still felt good. She welcomed it. He walked towards the kitchen. Even in her old home, the kitchen had always been their favorite place to sit, laugh, converse, and on occasion, other things.

"Would you like something to eat?"

He declined, "but I'd like something to drink if you have it."

"Sure, iced tea, water, Merlot, Corona."

"Corona, please."

She could feel his eyes following her as she nervously walked to the refrigerator. "Glass? Thad."

"I'm strictly a bottle man, baby. You know that."

She sat beside him. After about ten minutes of laughing and awkward conversation, they ran out of the small talk, falling silent. She looked at him fixedly. She had to ask. "What happened, Thad? How could you just walk out and leave me? How could you say you loved me and do what you did? Not taking my calls. Ignoring me? Living with another woman? If you didn't want me, why did you get married in the first place?"

Thad looked anguished, "I don't know, Essie. Things were different when we were dating. When we got married, things changed, especially as far as money was concerned. Then there was the problem with my children. I felt constricted. You expected so much from me. I couldn't live up to your expectations, so I left."

"Constricted?" she repeated, "Money problems? Thad, when we were dating, I was responsible for myself solely. Occasionally you would help, but I handled my own responsibilities. When we married, I expected more from you. You were my husband, not my boyfriend. It was your responsibility to do more. I did my part as a wife; and regarding money, we had a few financial issues, not problems. But that's no reason to end a marriage and start cheating on me. And as far as your children are concerned, I've always accepted and treated them as my own. So, what are you talking about?"

She could feel herself getting angry. She grew quiet. It was time to be silent. She had to bridle her tongue. Otherwise, she would explode! She listened attentively as her husband spoke tearfully, honestly, dishonestly about their break-up. He gave a hundred excuses for leaving but not one reason. She felt hurt again. Before the conversation was over, it was apparent that Thad was gone not because of her but because of him. Although he said one thing, his actions displayed another. She realized that he wanted the benefits of marriage with the life of a single man, coming and going when he pleased, spending his money as he wished to, not having to answer to anyone, including her.

"What am I supposed to do about this situation, Thad? Shall I continue to live apart from my husband with not even a little communication on your part? You say you love me, but you're not making any attempt to be with me. You don't even have your own place. You live with her! How long should I put my life on pause for you, Thad? How long? I'm a young woman. I want a husband here with me. Not one who cavorts here and there." It was obvious that her sin of infidelity was exacting its payback on her. Now she knew how Sonny felt, torn apart.

She remembered a Bible verse, 1 Cor. 13:11: *When I was a child, I spake as a child, I understood as a child, I thought as a child: but when I became a man, I put away childish things.* Thad had not put away his childish things, nor was he ready to be the husband he had vowed to be. He was an immature boy in the body of a 45-year-old man.

"Thad," she asked finally, "what is the purpose for your visit?"

"I wanted to see you and say, I'm sorry. I'm not ready to be with you now, Essie; I have some things to work out for me."

"What about our marriage?"

"I'm just not ready."

"Just not ready," the words resonated in her mind. "Is it because of that woman you live with?" She asked angrily.

"I don't live with anyone. I live alone."

"She knew he was lying. That is what he was, a liar. For the first time in six months, she was sorry that she'd ever met him. Not because he didn't love her, but because even after she divorced Sonny, Thad still had no intention of being a husband. He viewed their relationship as little more than a glorified liaison. In short, an intimate snatch and grab.

As far as she was concerned, this conversation and their relationship were over. She had married a man who didn't know the first thing about commitment. His life with women had never amounted to more than bogus instances of pomp and circumstance. Why should marriage to her be any different? She had opened the door to her heart to Thaddeus Tisdale, but instead of a good man entering, his lies walked in. Now it was time for both of them to leave.

Get to Stepping!

* * * * *

On any given night, you could hear her crying into her pillow. On any given day, anguished, bloodshot eyes would greet you instead of her usual radiant smile. Her pain tugged at your heartstrings, but this was all a part of healing, and it had to take place. On the day she filed for divorce, she vowed that that would be her last night crying over Thaddeus Tisdale, and it was. Although his name sometimes crossed her mind, especially when acquaintances asked what happened, she could honestly say he no longer occupied a space in her heart. And little-by-little, between her own strength, prayer, and good friends, she returned to the Esmeralda that she once knew.

"Essie…"

She could hear someone calling her but saw no one. The market was always busy on the weekend, and if a person were not right near you, sometimes you couldn't hear.

"Essie."

She thought she heard a man's voice. Scanning the crowd, she saw Vie approaching, talking on her cell phone. "Was that you calling me?"

"No."

"Essie."

She heard it again. Looking from left to right, she still saw no one, "Vie, I know you hear that, don't you?"

"Hear what?"

"Vie, a man, calling my name. It sounds like…," Essie turned around and faced her past. A smiling Sonny stood before her. He, too, was holding a cell phone.

"Were you talking to…?" she began. There was no need to finish the question. She knew this was Vie's handy work.

"Hey, Sonny… What are you doing here?" She could hardly contain herself. She felt like a schoolgirl seeing her high school sweetheart for the first time in years. Sonny Valentine always had a way of making her genuinely blush.

"Oh… I'm just picking up a few things."

"Lunchmeat?" She questioned.

"Yep, that too. So how are you, Essie?"

"Fine, Sonny… Just fine."

"I called you several times at the café. Didn't Dexter give you the message?"

"He did, but you know how busy it gets sometimes."

"Were you too busy or not interested?"

"Truthfully, Sonny, neither. Too embarrassed."

He took her hand, "Your brother told me about the divorce."

"Really?"

"Yes, really. I can't say that I'm sorry to hear it either. I'm glad you're free."

"Listen, Sonny," she began, "If you're going to start…"

He cut her off in mid-sentence. "Essie, I'm not going to start anything. I'm just saying I'm glad you're single again. So am I."

"I've done a lot of growing during these past two years. I've been attending both anger management and counseling for months. I go to church often. I've changed. I'm a different person. A better person. I've sent my third world customs back to the third world. I'm sorry that I treated you so badly. You didn't deserve that. I was a... how do you say it in English? An ohgree?"

"An ohgree? Do you mean, ogre, Sonny?"

"Yes, that's it, an ogre. I'd love you to see how much I've grown. Maybe we could have dinner."

Essie could not believe this was Sonny. "Maybe," She responded, "on one condition."

"What is it?"

"Only if you promise to leave the past behind."

"I do," was his swift reply. "I've finally realized that what God has said is true, Essie."

"What's that?" she questioned.

He looked at her fixedly, "You know, in Proverbs 18:22. It says, *Whoso findeth a wife findeth a good thing, and obtaineth favour of the Lord.*"

I had a good wife in you, Essie, and I didn't appreciate the wonderfulness of you. God gave me favor when He gave me you. I was just too prideful and stupid to realize it. I'm so sorry. I'd really like to see where our paths lead. How about you?"

She could feel the tears welling in her eyes. *Oh yes,* she thought. Sonny Valentine was still the full package. He grabbed her and kissed her on the cheek. He had always kissed her. And like the old days, when she hugged him, he hugged her back and held her tight, real tight. He was still a man to reckon with. And like Sonny, she too was up to the challenge to love again. Sonny was opening the door to his heart and inviting her to come in. She entered… and stayed.

Welcome Home

CHAPTER 3

He Held My Hand

The growling in my stomach confirmed Charlotte's lateness for our lunch. My entire morning consisted of rush, rush, rush, and no food. I turned to signal the waiter for a morsel when in walked Charlotte, my long-time friend.

"Charlotte, you look fabulous!"

Charlotte took her seat and apologized for her laggard arrival.

"Don't worry about that!" I said, "Just answer two questions: How are you handling things? And how do you look so fantastic?"

Charlotte blushed, "Well," she said, "things are better now. And regarding my looks, don't I look the same?"

"Are you kidding? I can't get over how you look!"

"How's that?" she asked, reading the menu and me too.

"Refreshed," I said. You're glowing from the inside out. Less than a year ago, you were an emotional and physical wreck! Blotchy skin, thinning hair, crying for weeks on end. And rightly so. The miscarriage took its toll on you. And then the baby's father pulled that *'fifty ways to leave your lover'* routine by walking out on you. You were going through a lot, Char. That's why I called you all of the time. But look at you now! Did you get a facelift?"

"Heavens, no! Charlotte exclaimed! Besides, I couldn't afford it anyway."

"What then?" I asked, "Counseling... medication... A new man?"

"No. Nothing like that," Charlotte said with a smile. "Quite simply, *He held my hand.*"

"Who held your hand?" I asked.

"Jesus."

"Jesus who?"

"Jesus Christ."

"Jesus Christ! You mean like in the Bible?"

"Yep. Like in the Bible."

"Wait a minute. Char. You're telling me that you were going through extreme depression, hurt, and the loss of a child, and the only help you had, **was Jesus?** Puhleeeeeeeze!"

"That's exactly what I'm telling you, Vicky. He pulled me through."

My befuddlement showed, *how could someone you can't see...don't hear...and can't talk to help you get over anything?*

Charlotte sipped her tea. "This is a nice place, Vicky. Thanks for taking me to lunch."

"You've always been there for me, Char. Besides, I just got my tax return. Now, back to this Jesus thing. My mother's always saying, 'The Lord this, the Lord that,' but is He?"

"Is He what? Vicky."

"Is He the same person as Jesus?"

"The very same one."

"But what's so special about Jesus, Char? I remember reading somewhere, "Take your problems to Jesus. He'll work them out.""

"Well, do you?" Charlotte asked.

"Do I what?"

"Do you take your problems to Him?"

"Of course not! How you can take problems to someone you don't see, can't hear, and can't touch. What are you talking to, AIR?"

"No, Vicky. It's a spiritual connection. It's something hard to explain. Everyone has to experience God for themselves because it's a personal relationship."

"Come with me to Bible study tomorrow night, Vicky. It's not long at all, only one hour. And if you don't want to stay, we'll leave. The pastor and the members are welcoming. You'll get to eat some really fantastic baked goods. And guess who we'll be talking about?"

"Don't tell me, Jesus. Right?" We laughed.

Bible study, I thought, on the way home. This could be the answer to my million-dollar question. Who is this Jesus, and why are those who know Him so happy? Maybe learning more about Him could help me to understand why I wasn't happy? I loved my job, shared a fabulous home with my mother, and unlike most of my friends, I was happily single. But something gnawed at my innards. And at 33 years old, I still didn't know what it was.

After a good night's sleep and a productive day at work, I looked forward to going to Bible study. I looked at my watch. Oops... running late, Charlotte arrived at 6:30 to whisk me away.

The small church classroom was packed when we arrived. "Do this many people usually come to Bible study?" I inquired.

"Usually."

"*There must be something really special about Jesus,*" I said to myself, as we took our seats. We both listened attentively as Pastor Jerome spoke. I wanted to ask questions but felt a little intimidated.

"Char...pssst...Char." Will people look at me like I'm stupid if I ask a question?"

"Of course not," she replied. That's why we're all here. To ask questions and learn the Bible.``

My reluctance to raise my hand was apparent. First up, then down ...Then down and up. Finally, I said, "Pastor, may I ask a few questions?"

"By all means," he acknowledged.

"Where did Jesus come from?"

"From Heaven."

"How do you know?"

"Scripture tells us."

"What Scripture?"

"1 John 4:9 and 1 John 4:14 – read it."

"⁹In this was manifested the love of God toward us, because that God sent his only begotten Son into the world, that we might live through him. ¹⁰Herein is love, not that we loved God, but that he loved us and sent His Son to be the propitiation for our sins. ¹⁴And, we have seen and do testify that the Father sent the Son to be the Savior of the world."

"Well...I'm not entirely sure what that means, but I do have another question: If Jesus was God – how could He be man?"

"Good question Vicky. Turn to John 1:14. What does it say?"

"It says...And the Word was made flesh, and dwelt among us, (and we beheld his glory, the glory as of the only begotten of the Father,) full of grace and truth."

My probing queries continued until all shyness faded and excitement reigned. Even though the class was extended by twenty minutes because of my questions, my classmates seemed to enjoy my exuberance as much as I did.

"Will I see you next week, Vicky?"

"Certainly, Pastor." I think he knew another soul was about to be saved.

"Did you like it?" Charlotte questioned.

"Yes, I did! And in case you didn't know, Char, this was my first Bible study."

"Oh." She coyly replied. "I wouldn't have guessed."

I responded with one word. "Liar."

Mother was in bed when I arrived home. "Mom," I yelled. "You'll never believe where I just came from!"

"Where, honey?"

"Bible Study."

"Bible Study," she repeated as she repositioned her bed pillows. Sometimes my mother ached so badly. Many times, she'd grimace in pain, but she never complained.

"Are you feeling bad, mom?" she said, "no," but I knew better.

"These tired bones need rest, honey, but hearing your wonderful news makes me feel much better. My Lord...my Lord," she said, "Vicky at Bible study."

"I went with Charlotte. We had lunch yesterday. I asked how she was dealing with her loss, and she told me, "Jesus." You know I had no idea what she was talking about."

"What about now?" Mother asked.

"Let's just say I'm getting a better understanding of His purpose."

"Well... I guess that's a step in the right direction, honey. I've been trying to get you to go to bible study for years. Sometimes it doesn't matter how you take the medicine as long as it gets in your system."

My mother's prayers were different that night. I could hear her saying, "Thank you, Lord. That Vicky would know you before I leave this earth has been my prayer. You're answering it now.

I became a regular at Bible study. And without realizing it, one week turned into two, two into four, and in a flash, two years of consistent attendance had gone by. And it was fun! I was changing. I knew it. My mother knew it. Charlotte knew it. But most of all, HE knew it! My life took a new turn. Old feelings of discontentment were a distant memory. I was happy!

Shortly after I became saved, my mother passed away. It was a hard time for me. I cried many nights because my best friend was gone, but I wasn't alone. I remembered Charlotte's words, **"He Held my Hand."** I finally knew what she meant because now, HE was holding mine.

Several months later, a neighbor called me as I entered my home. I turned to see Jesse waving from across the street.

"Hi, Vicky, it's so good to see you. How have you been?"

"Fine, Jesse. Just fine."

"I'm sorry about your mother. I know how close you were."

"Thanks, Jess."

"….But Vicky, what happened to you?"

"Whatta you mean, Jess?"

The last time I saw you – you looked sad and depressed because you were grieving. But now, you look amazing! Did you get counseling or attend a bereavement group?"

"No...Not at all."

"Were you on medication?"

"No. Nothing like that!"

"Well, *what* then? I need to snap out of this funk that I'm in. Please tell me your secret."

"Very simply, Jess. He Held My Hand."

"Who held your hand?"

I smiled… Here we go again!

CHAPTER 4

Internal Grave

Richard didn't realize it, but because of him, Candice was dead. Although there were no traces of blood and no weapons found at the scene, she had ceased to exist because of him. Bit-by-bit, he siphoned her emotions with indiscreet rendezvous and encounters. With each kiss stolen from her and bestowed on another. With each lie, he told. No, Richard didn't realize it, but week-after-week, month-after-month, he had obliterated her, and now, Candice, his wife of four years, was dead.

Though physically, she was still alive, his disloyalties had assassinated everything in her that mattered - her heart, love, passion, even the belief that he ever loved her. All were now buried in an internal grave, which she visited daily, each time leaving a piece of herself.

Richard had reduced what she thought was a loving marriage to a tainted version of happily-ever-after built on lies, deceit, and adultery? She laughed when he angrily approached her, ranting like a child. "I feel like a prisoner in this house."

"A prisoner?" she fired back. Wobbling her head in astonishment.

"Yes, Candice," He continued. "A prisoner! I'm afraid to go around the corner to the store because you don't trust me!"

"Trust you?" She repeated, "How can I? Less than six months ago, you cheated on me. And I forgave you. Since then, I've caught you on how many dating sites? Not trusting you, Richard, is an understatement! At least twice a week, you disappear, and I have no idea where you go. So, tell me, Richard, whose fault is that? At this point, trust is out the window. And you put it there!"

"I'm not saying that I didn't cause it, Candice. And yes, maybe I have made a few mistakes. No…let me rephrase that - I have made multiple mistakes. But you're still my wife, and I do love you. I want our marriage to work. Can't you understand that?"

Richard thought for a moment and then grew silent. He realized that Candice had hit him with a verbal knockout with her last statement. And like any punch-drunk fighter, he was down for the count, unable to stand.

She stood at the ready but said nothing as he quietly walked away. She wanted to believe his "I Love Yous," but to her, they were nothing more than meaningless, empty words that she'd heard several times before. Everyone knows that love is an action word, she thought, but his prior actions consisted of deceit and infidelity. Love for her was nowhere in sight.

On more than one occasion, she had visited a lawyer to file for divorce, but she never made it past the first meeting. She knew all too well that although her mind was ready to end the relationship, her heart wasn't. Richard was the love of her life. Her partner forever. She was shocked to realize that those feelings were not only one-sided but also a big, fat lie!

Two times in the past, she had put him out of the house, only to accept him back a month or so later. Richard gave her no peace during their separations. Early morning calls of "Good morning, Candice" were followed by afternoon calls of "What are you doing?" And late-night calls of "Can I come over?" His "I'm sorrys" were like scratched records always getting stuck on *sorry...sorry...sorry.* But still, she'd play them over-and-over again.

His offenses with other women were not mere dalliances, but sexual interludes – that, when discovered, left her devastated. Breathless. Crushed. Dead. But despite his reckless indiscretions, her embers of love still burned for him. *Matters of the heart are always painful*, she thought, especially when it's your heart that's breaking.

Her husband's unfaithful transgressions had revealed themselves, and now he wanted forgiveness for his wrongdoings, *but am I ready to forgive?* She wondered, *Could what was dead now resurrect?* As far as she knew, there had only been one person resurrected from the dead, and His name surely *wasn't* Candice.

Her eyes opened early the next morning with thoughts of the church bake sale on her mind. Lemon pie, pound cake, oatmeal raisin cookies - recipes for each of them swirled in her head - but not one ounce of flour, sugar, or other necessary ingredients sat in her cabinets. She glanced at the clock sitting on her night table. *6:45 a.m.* She looked to her right-no Richard. *I bet he slept on the couch,* she thought. The clock was buzzing now. She forced herself out of bed. The church flea market and bake sale would begin at nine o'clock. The thought amused her of a bake sale with no baked goods. Although she laughed at the idea, she knew the church members wouldn't.

She called out to Richard. No answer. After twenty minutes of getting ready, she made her way downstairs and peered into the living room—no Richard. *He probably went for coffee.* She grabbed her keys and purse and was out the door.

Her shiny new car sat in the driveway. She made a mental timeline as she entered. A quick stop at the market – then back home – begin baking – be finished by 8:30 – be at church by 8:45. *It sounds good,* she thought. "What's that on the dashboard?" She asked herself. "A note?"

Dear Candice, I had to leave early. I'm helping out at the church. I'll see you there. Please know that I'm so sorry and that I love you. I want our marriage to work. See you at church. Love Richard.

P.S. I put gas in the car for you.

"Richard," she said aloud, "just when I'm ready to discount you - you do something endearing." She then started her car - and was off.

The church grounds were bustling activity when she arrived. Tents, tables, vendors, and people were everywhere! Children were playing, dogs were running, patrons were buying. It was going to be a good day. Twenty minutes after she put her famous lemon pound cakes on display for two dollars a slice - she could see Richard approaching.

"Hey, Candice."

"Hi, Richard."

"You okay?" He asked.

"Why wouldn't I be?"

"No reason. I was just asking. Did you see my note?"

"Yes. Thanks for the gas."

"Candice..."

"Yes. Richard."

"Do you have about thirty minutes after the bake sale to meet with me and Pastor Reuben?"

"You and Pastor...for what, Richard?"

"He'd like to speak with us."

"About what?"

"About us, Candice. About our marriage."

"You spoke with the Pastor about our marriage?

"Yes. I've been counseling with Pastor for almost two months."

His words stunned her, "Almost two months?"

"Yes. Twice a week for almost two months.

"Oh my gosh!" She thought, *"That's where he's been disappearing to."*

"So, will you meet with us?" he asked again.

"Ummm."

"C'mon, Candice. Can't you see I'm trying?" He could see the wheels turning behind her eyes. "Please, honey."

"I don't know, Richard. I don't want to give you any false hopes."

"Look, Candice. I have no expectations. At this point, all I have is hope. Please come."

"Okay," she finally said, "As soon as the bake sale is over, I'll stop in."

Richard smiled, kissed her on the cheek, and then disappeared into the bustling crowd.

As each hour passed, Candice played the video of their marriage over-and-over in her mind. Had she played a part in the distressed state of their marriage? Even her husband's infidelity? She had to be truthful. Richard was always a loving husband, but was she a loving wife? She hesitated for a moment. If being honest, she realized that she hadn't made time for him in almost a year. It wasn't his fault that they were like ships passing in the night. It was hers. Her busy work schedule left her gone half of the time and exhausted the other half. Many times, Richard offered her the opportunity to work part-time or not at all. After all, he made more than enough money to support them comfortably. Still, to her, corporate marketing wasn't a part-time job, and being a stay-at-home mother and wife wasn't her cup of tea. Many times Richard talked about starting a family, but five years later, she was still on birth control, and the thought of getting off had never entered her mind.

She remembered how many times he'd call her during the day just to say, "I Love You." She then also remembered how many times she'd eschew him with "I'm busy, Richard. I'll call you back," but she never did. Some nights he'd prepare a romantic dinner with her favorite foods, but she'd come in too tired to eat. Other times, he'd run a warm bath for her with candles, but she'd drain the tub, blow out the candles and take a shower. Every so often, he'd schedule a get-away weekend to give her a break – but on the day of, she'd have an excuse, and he'd have to cancel the trip - often losing money. Then she remembered times when he'd do this, or he'd do that just to make things pleasant for her. But she never appreciated the niceties, the care, or the concern.

She cringed when she thought of the last time that they had been intimate. To her recollection, snow was on the ground. Presently, it was summer. She had to face it, although Richard should have lassoed his libido and exercised restraint, long days followed by longer nights never made good bedfellows, and she too was a culprit in this marital faux pas. At that moment, she asked God, *how could she have been so selfish? How could she have maltreated her husband so?* She then asked the ultimate question, *what now?*

"Hello, Pastor."

"Hello, Candice. It's nice to see you."

"Likewise."

Upon seeing his wife, Richard rose to greet her. "Hi, Baby. Thanks for coming."

Candice smiled.

"Do you know why we're here, Candice?" asked Pastor Reuben as he took a seat behind his desk.

"Yes, to discuss the marital problems between Richard and me.

"That's right."

Candice looked at her husband, "quite honestly," she said, "I didn't know that you have been coming here for counseling, Richard. Why didn't you tell me?"

"Because I have caused you so much hurt, Candice, that I wanted to get myself right before involving you. I wanted you to know that I am serious and that our marriage means everything to me.

"Yes, Candice," interjected Pastor Reuben, "Richard has been coming here faithfully. He's been..."

Before any of them knew it, almost three hours of conversation had passed. During that time, tears flowed, honestly was revealed, secrets were unmasked, hope was alive, misdeeds forgave, and a crumbling marriage was on the road to restoration.

On that day, Richard made a forceful declaration, "Candice, believe me, this will be the last day that we'll be in this office discussing my marital transgressions. I promise to be the husband that God intended me to be."

Candice looked at her husband and began to cry, "No, Richard, it is I who need to apologize to you, as well. I have not been the wife that you deserve. I've been selfish, self-centered, and inconsiderate in many ways. I'm ashamed of the way that I've treated you. So today, I'm asking for forgiveness too. Will you forgive me, Richard?"

Richard kneeled in front of her and hugged her tightly. She felt their hearts beating in unison. Then, it happened! For the first time in a long time, she hugged him back. They were bonding again. The emotional purge between them was unlike anything either had felt before. Her heart was *telling* her that what was *once dead between them* was being resurrected. And she was listening.

Candice smiled. She knew that the visits to her internal grave were over. As she grabbed her purse, Richard grabbed her hand. They exited Pastor Reuben's office and shut the door on the past forever.

CHAPTER 5

How Many Cooks Are in This Kitchen?

My grandmother gave birth to seven charming and interesting daughters. Though she had five sons, her daughters (my aunts) are the ones that I'm going to talk about now. So, get ready to meet them all!

The "Littleton Girls" consisted of my aunts: Willamena, Alma, Gina (my mother), Glynnis, Lovette, Beatrice (who was the youngest), and Lillian. Neighborhood girls loved and enjoyed their friendship, while neighborhood boys loved them for everything that they wanted but couldn't have. Remember, my aunts had five rough, tough, well-liked brothers. And they all could fight! I'm talking about the girls!

They grew up having a family life that many children desire; a loving, safe home, a stable environment, a drug-free neighborhood, house rules, behavior rules, deliciously prepared meals, daily chores. And when needed, a good, old-fashioned spanking, which grandmother gave more freely than desired.

As my aunts matured and evolved into womanhood, they developed many individual talents that ranged from designing clothes to home decorating, to whatever other God-given gifts they possessed and enjoyed. Even though each was unique in their way, they had one thing in common. They could burn in the kitchen. Grandma Littleton had taught them well.

My mother was a chef and a culinary genius. Aunt Alma was a restaurateur, Aunts Glynnis and Beatrice were caterers, Aunt Willamena was the best with Northern fried chicken. Aunt Lilly couldn't cook at all. And Aunt Lovette, well, let's say that even in her 70s, she was still evolving as a cook. Holidays with them were tasty feasts because they all brought something special to family food gatherings. And we've got the bodies to prove it!

My aunts would prepare Thanksgiving and Christmas dinners in my grandmother's kitchen. They would fill the room with love, laughter, and lengthy disagreements about how many eggs to put into this… or how much salt to put into that. Sometimes they'd argue so loudly that my grandmother, the Grand Dame, would intervene and show them what real cooking was all about. Her favorite question was, "How many cooks are in this kitchen?" Translation: "I'm here now. Be quiet!" Whenever the Grand Dame would enter the kitchen, silence would fall, and meal preparation would continue in a hushed and rational manner. By the end of the day, the entire family would sit down and enjoy a meal fit for royalty.

Just as their recipes varied from making sweet potato pie to stuffing a turkey, so varied their methods on what it took to make a good marriage. Often one would say, "I wouldn't take that from my husband." While another might reply, "Your husband's worse!" But no matter how much they disagreed, one thing was sure; each truly believed that the main ingredient needed for a good marriage was God. My aunts believed that without God at the center of their marriages, none of them would have, nor could have, endured the trials that people in love face to ensure the longevity of marriage.

In some way, each of them had a marriage that wouldn't rise, wasn't sweet, wasn't tender, didn't have enough spice, was over-cooked, or was just plain-old-tough! But no matter what their marriages lacked, my grandmother would always tell them "to pray and put God at the forefront of their marriage." Prayer was her mainstay recipe for a marriage that lasted over 60 years and undoubtedly, endured the test of time.

Gina

Whenever my mother threw a party, everyone wanted to be there. Guests would mark their calendars, purchase outfits, buy new shoes and call their dancing partner (if they had one); because Gina was having a party. And to many, it was the party-of-the-year that no one wanted to miss.

To partygoers, Gina's home was fabulous and inviting. She was the quintessential hostess among hostesses. Her food was delicious and beautifully orchestrated; the drinks were top-shelf and free. Her guests were friendly, good-looking people. Her DJ was always on point with the music, and the dance floor was always full. Gina was gracious, entertaining, and fabulous!

She was a regal woman who enjoyed her life. But those who truly knew Gina also knew that her life wasn't always so happy; or so carefree. And if asked, she'd be the first to admit that her early years with my father were quite different.

Although her marriage lasted a little more than 33 years, my mother's happily-ever-after remained crippled by a husband addicted to heroin. Was my father a secure provider? Yes, he was. He provided her with every luxury a woman could want. Was he a loving father? Definitely! We lived well, ate well, were disciplined well, and we were loved well. My brother and I had the best of what our parents could afford. And though I never mastered the runway, I even went to charm school because I was so clumsy.

My brother and I had it easy, mainly because we were young and unaware of my father's addiction. My mother suffered in silence while enduring twenty-five years of drug abuse by my father; twenty-five years of on-the-wagon, off-the-wagon. Twenty-five years of the pain that comes from living with a drug-addicted spouse. Many times throughout their marriage, my mother wanted to call it quits. She even separated from him several times, but as a woman in love and wanting to keep the family together, she'd always take him back; and things would be beautiful until the next time.

Though my father wasn't her first husband, he was her first and only true love. They were childhood, neighboring sweethearts, loving each other from afar. Their serious dating started after the dissolution of my mother's first marriage at age 17. She would have married my father first, but rumor has it that while my father was thinking about marriage, someone else was asking, and she accepted.

By age 18, my mother divorced husband number 1 and was married to my father. But marriage to my father, Ruby, as his family lovingly called him, was what lifetimes are made of. It bore lots of love, forgiveness, stick-to-itiveness, raising children alone (if necessary), and holding down the fort until the cavalry arrived. She was an exemplary wife, even if he wasn't an exemplary husband. But through it all, I had a praying grandmother.

Blessed with a fantastic job, my mother always strived to do better and to be better. In his way, my father did too. My parents saw that my brother and I were educated, well-rounded, spiritually adept, and exposed to the finer things at an early age. As a family, we were happy, but like my Aunt Alma, my mother, too, was crippled by the pain of a dysfunctional marriage, and she needed an outlet.

She, just like Aunt Alma, became a weekend gambler. Every weekend they would invent and reinvent creative stories explaining disappearances that lasted until 12:00 and 1:00 a.m. Each Friday or Saturday, like Siamese twins, they would slip out to play poker in hopes of relieving internal pain and winning some money.

Though she played poker like a pro on Fridays and Saturdays, every Sunday would find my mother in church asking God to save her and my father. Unbeknownst to me, I had a praying grandmother, who like my mother, prayed for the same thing.

For years, my mother provided the aegis to aid my father in his struggle with addiction. She traveled with him physically and emotionally during his vicious cycle of Methadone clinics, rehabs, counseling, and jail. Jail, counseling, rehabs, and Methadone clinics. She lived by the credo, *"Work with me, and I'll work with you."* She swallowed her pride, and with him, she attended every meeting, every counseling session, and every 12-step program in hopes that he would stay on track.

One day my father was arrested for possession of drugs and spent seven months in jail. It was then that my mother decided that she could no longer ride on his merry-go-round of addiction. She secured a realtor, sold our small house, and secretly looked for a new residence.

The move was a total surprise to my brother and me. We arrived home from school with open mouths and wide eyes when we saw the movers. We had but one expression among us... SHOCK!

"Where are we going?" We asked simultaneously, as my mother appeared in the hallway. She simply replied, *"To our new home."*

"What about Daddy?" Was our next question.

To which she replied, *"Don't worry about Daddy."*

I was in 9th grade, and my brother in the 8th, and we were comfortable! We loved our schools. We loved our friends. We loved our lives, but that didn't matter. We were whisked off to our new home, grumbling all the way. Although we didn't see Daddy for over three months, once a week, the phone operator would call and say, *"Collect call from…"*

Upon his release from jail, my mother was the first person that Daddy contacted. In less than a month, his weekly visits with us turned into daily ones. Soon regular visits turned into nightly ones. Then nightly visits turned into weekend ones. And weekend visits turned into… well, you know the rest. A short time later, he was living with us and in full daddy-mode: dictating orders and laying down rules, handing out punishments with one-hand while providing allowances with the other. He obtained a well-paying job at a steel mill, and almost immediately, we were back on track as a family.

Although he didn't go to church, my mother, brother, and I would go faithfully. When my brother went away to private school, my mother and I continued going to church. We lit candles and prayed vigilantly for my father to stay off drugs. For a long while, he did, and life was good. But four years later, he was off-the-wagon again.

I was sometimes uncertain of what caused my father's miasmic haze, but my mother knew for sure. Daddy had relapsed. But this time, there were no Methadone clinics, no more rehabs, and no more counseling - only prayers. One day my mother said to me, *"Don't worry about your father. God will take him off the drugs."* If my mother believed it, then so did I.

One day my father was very distraught. Later I found out that his childhood friend, who was more like a brother, had succumbed to a drug overdose and died. My father loved him dearly. It was the death of his friend that stopped my father from using drugs. He didn't stop immediately, but once he finished, he never used them again. He started going to church with us and thanking God for his wife and his deliverance from drugs. Finally, he was free from the bondage that held him captive for more than twenty-five years.

Five years later, a car accident altered the course of my father's life. A woman ran a stop sign, striking his car. His head hit the windshield. A month later, he developed two brain aneurysms; one was operable, one wasn't. He died within two years. Before he died, he thanked God for blessing him with a praying wife and two beautiful children.

Several years later, my mother met someone, fell in love, and re-married. Although she loved him, and their marriage lasted for almost twenty years, it was Ruby (my father) that her heart walked through time with. In her heart, even if she married a thousand times, Ruby could never be replaced. My mother passed away in 2002, but her memory, the love that we shared, her teachings, and her eloquence will remain with us forever.

Alma

A devoted woman of God married to a weekend alcoholic. That's right! A weekend alcoholic. Her husband, my uncle, worked hard every day. But on Friday nights, he'd leave work and beeline to the nearest liquor store.

Uncle Johnny was a logical drunk who rationalized his drinking. Since he didn't use drugs and because his liquor wasn't expensive, he could drink as much as he wanted. And drink, he did! After work on Fridays, he would drink and drink until Sunday (his sobering-up day). Sunday night, he'd recuperate, and Monday would find him back at work, without another drop of alcohol until the next Friday.

Alcohol was Uncle's other woman, and his body paid the price to indulge her; for he was extremely skinny. I often thought that if someone oiled him up and then tried to hug him, he'd probably slip right through their arms. He was just that thin.

Uncle loved Port wine because of its many benefits. Aside from lifting him to a higher state of unconsciousness, it was easy to obtain, legal, financially feasible. In no way did it economically deprive his family. Remember, "He was a logical drunk." Though his weekend binges were of little consequence to him, they burdened Aunt Alma with unbearable stress. She could hide many things from their six children, but tears and a heavy heart were too painful to hide.

Aunt Alma threatened to leave him several times, but she never did. She truly believed in 'till death do you part.' Aside from that, she had six children, and a single-parent household was out of the question. As uncle's alcoholism progressed, so did his jealousy. He monitored my aunt's comings-and-goings like a guard dog. Her home and marriage became an unbearable prison until the day she taught herself to play poker.

Rumor has it that my shy aunt became quite the gambler. Many weekends' while uncle lay home in a drunken stupor, Aunt Alma and my mother would sneak out and gamble. They'd play cards with neighbors until the wee hours of the morning. Aunt Alma felt justified because if he could drink, she could play cards. And play cards, she did. The more he drank, the more she gambled.

My aunt didn't worry about the care of her children because her mother-in-law lived with them. Many of Aunt Alma's home departures were successful; however, her returns, more often than not, were often met with opposition. Uncle would be up, waiting, and ready to get physical. Their pattern of drinking, gambling, and fighting continued for years, but like I said, "I had a praying grandmother," who took the problems of her daughter and son-in-law before the Lord and placed them on the altar.

One day Aunt Alma was gambling until 3:00 a.m. She went home to her sleeping children, the snores of her drunken husband, and the guilt that engulfed her. Overwhelmed with emotional despair, she sat in the living room and cried. The cycle of drinking and gambling had taken its toll. Aunt Alma fell to her knees and asked God for help. It was her first real encounter with the Lord. And according to her, God revealed that as long as she gambled, her husband would never stop drinking. She prayed and asked God to remove the gambling spirit from her. Two months later, God moved Aunt Alma away from her gambling friends into a much nicer neighborhood. Though uncle's drinking continued, she never played poker again.

One Saturday, Aunt Alma and her husband came over to visit my mother. As usual, he was drunk, and as usual, she protested - but her protests were to no avail. He paid her no mind as he guzzled his bottle of Port. She helped my mother with dishes as she sang the song, 'On the Street Where You Live.' Hearing this song sent my uncle into a frenzy; he came into the kitchen and started arguing with her, implying that she was singing this song because she was secretly seeing someone on our block.

She eschewed his complaints and told him, *"the liquor was making him act crazy."* He paid her no mind, flew into a drunken rage, and struck her in the face with a glass. Blood was everywhere! My mother started screaming, I started running, and Aunt Alma started crying. I quickly ran upstairs and peeked down through the railing. I still can't stand the sight of blood. My father, blazing with fury, appeared from nowhere and jumped into Superman mode. He punched my uncle twice; the first punch knocked my uncle from the living room, out of the screen door, and onto the porch. The second punch knocked him over the outside railing, which broke when he fell into it and onto the front lawn. He was out cold. But guess what? Even though he was unconscious and lying on his back, uncle never spilled a drop of the Port wine, which he held in his hand.

When he sobered up, my uncle had a complete nervous breakdown. Even though Aunt Alma was okay and suffered just a few minor scratches, the thought that he could have killed or marred his wife permanently – was too much for him to bear. The deed sent him over the edge. Instead of going to jail, my uncle was admitted to a mental institution for six months of therapy and detoxification.

During that time, Aunt Alma always prayed for God to heal and deliver him from the spirit of alcoholism that had possessed him for so long.

She prayed that her husband would grow to become a true man of God. Several times a week, she would visit him at the hospital. He was in therapy; she was in therapy; both were in treatment and trying to heal. She was willing to do whatever it took to bring them back to a normal and healthy life.

During one of her visits, Uncle Johnny told her that while praying in his room, "he saw a white light appear from nowhere." He continued to say, "That this light comforted him and began to minister to his spirit."

"Do you think it was God?" she asked.

He didn't know, but he knew two things for sure: 1. that he was truly_sorry for what he had done to her and their family, and 2. that he would never drink again.

When he was released several months later, the first person he came to visit was my father. He thanked my father for the two punches that saved his life.

My aunt and her husband started worshiping at the Seventh Day Adventist Church. They sought the Lord together and found Him. He became a minister, and she became an evangelist. Today they have been married for more years than I can remember, and he has never touched another drink. Though she's still capable of playing cards like a pro, she hasn't played cards for over thirty years. Praise God.

Lovette

The only words to describe the first half of my aunt's marriage are abuse, abuse, and more abuse. Mental, physical, and emotional abuse. For years, she endured an iniquitous cycle of whippings, slaps, and punches from her husband, regularly. Not only did he keep her pregnant, but he also provided physical chastisement if she got out of line.

She dropped out of high school and married her childhood sweetheart at fifteen years old. By age sixteen, she had her first child and two black eyes. Her husband, a mildly attractive light-skinned man, had a temper that was only rivaled by his vanity and chauvinism. Uncle Tee (short for Theodore) could come and go as he pleased but wouldn't allow her to move from the front doorsteps of their home. And the worst part was that - she listened!!

Aunt Lovette was then - and is now - a quiet, mild-mannered woman who married a man who was the total opposite. Although he wasn't a drug user or an alcoholic, he, for a long time, was plagued with another type of impediment. ABUSE.

I don't know much about their early life because I wasn't around. Still, according to family murmurs and whispers, he treated her rather badly. Some have likened his treatment of her to that of a bad master and a dog. Come when I call. Do as I say. And wag your tail when you see me coming. And that is precisely what she did. My aunt never complained to her family about her treatment. She didn't have to. Each time a sister would see her, she'd either have a bump, lump, or bruise that wasn't there the week before. But she never complained. Auntie knew all too well that her brothers, without question, would inflict the same punishment on uncle that he had so readily bestowed.

By the time Aunt Lovette was 28, she had given birth to all four of her children. And like her mother before her, all four of them were being reared in the church. As my aunt matured into womanhood, she became a better wife, but my uncle wasn't a better husband. In his eyes, she was still the 15-year-old girl that he married thirteen years earlier. It was his adverse treatment, which forced her to seek God's face wholeheartedly. The longer they stayed married, the more ingratiated her and the children became in church. At least three nights a week, you'd find Aunt Lovette and the four Little-Lovette's occupying the first five seats - on the first row - at Cedar Baptist. It was a small, friendly, family-oriented church, and her mother-in-law was the assistant pastor. Oh yeah, Mr. Rockem-Sockem was the son of a preacher woman.

By the time my aunt was 33, she had experienced her first mild nervous breakdown. And though she didn't admit to it, her sisters knew that uncle was the cause. Aunt Lovette was a stay-at-home wife and mother who never had to work. She raised children, cleaned the house, cooked meals, packed lunches, and provided regular wifely dispensations because he was the love of her life.

On the other hand, Uncle worked hard, provided for his family, went to school, cavorted with the opposite sex, drank liquor, came home when he wanted, did what he wanted, and shall we say, 'socialized' when he wanted. But through it all, my grandmother prayed.

Don't get me wrong; life between the two of them wasn't all bad. In between their children's birth, my aunt and uncle managed to travel, dress like Siamese twins, attend family and social outings. And to my surprise, they even attended church together. But uncle still had a lot of growing to do.

When he was in his early 50's, Uncle Tee left my aunt and moved into an apartment by himself. What he said was, *"he wanted to concentrate on school without interference."* What he didn't say was, *"he wanted to be free. Not divorced, but unencumbered to come, go and socialize, as he pleased."*

Although he took care of his family financially, his leaving reeled my aunt into a state that left her physically weak, emotionally drained, and mentally fragile, but God never left her side; and neither did her sisters. Alma, Gina, Beatrice, Willamena, Lillian, and Glynnis were dutiful soldiers from beginning to end. They rallied round, dispensed medicine, cooked food, planned strategies, and policed the barracks, keeping Uncle Tee at bay until the appropriate time, but above all, they prayed vigilantly. It was the love of her sisters that helped to pull auntie through. Many times, she said, "children are wonderful, but there's a certain strength in sister-love, which children can't provide."

Within two years, Uncle Tee moved back home. Even though his punches and slaps had stopped some years earlier, his arrogance was at an all-time high. My aunt suffered one more nervous breakdown. But her children, now grown, took charge. Aunt Lovette stayed with a daughter until she reclaimed her strength and sanity, never to relinquish them again.

Shortly after he returned home, Uncle Tee's mother died. His devastation was beyond belief! Soon after that, his elder sister passed away, devastating him even more. It was through these deaths that uncle began to change. God was working on him.

We know that God does things in his own time. He blesses those He wants to bless and curses those He wants to curse. In my uncle's case, God blessed him with Prostate cancer. Yes, blessed him. And uncle's blessings were two-fold. Cancer forced him to rely on God and depend on his wife for help because he could do very little for himself. Initially, this made him very mean. But God had a plan. The meaner he became – the more he had to depend on my aunt, who never left his side. The longer she stood, the closer they became. God was tenderizing him in heart and spirit. Uncle no longer viewed his wife as the fifteen-year-old girl he had married 35 years earlier, but now, he saw her beauty as a full-grown woman of God for the first time. God was blossoming their relationship into what it was always meant to be; one of love, adoration, trust, and fidelity.

Today Auntie and Uncle are in their eighties. He is a minister and senior pastor of the church where his mother once ministered. She is an Evangelist and first lady. After 70 years of marriage, their relationship is loving and rock-solid.

Although Uncle still gives her a light slap from time-to-time, it's no longer to her face but rather to her still much-adored derriere. Because even after 70 years of marriage, he still likes the way it looks, but he loves the way it feels.

God is in the blessing business.

Willamena

What can you say about Aunt Willamena, or as we lovingly called her, Aunt Willie? There was probably no one in Philadelphia who could fry a better piece of chicken than my aunt. She'd get out the Lawry's Seasoned Salt along with her other special seasonings, and one bite would put you in chicken heaven.

Though she wasn't very refined and lacked my other aunts' social graces, sometimes she was funny as all-get-out and a joy to be around. My aunt had three rules for all nieces and nephews who entered her home. Rule #1. You had to address her properly in accordance with the time of day by saying, "good morning, good afternoon, or good evening, Aunt Willamena." Rule #2. Upon entering her home, all males had to remove their hats. Rule #3. If you knew how to, you had to play the card game p-knuckle with her. Frankly, playing p-knuckle was a requirement before you could leave her home. And she always had the cards locked and loaded and sitting on her dining room table, ready to go.

My aunt had five children: three boys and two girls. She was strict with all of them. So those who didn't vacate her home by way of marriage (namely the girls) left immediately after their high school diploma was received (namely the boys).

She was a tall, dark-skinned, large, and healthy woman, weighing every bit of 300 pounds. Her husband, my Uncle Milton, was the exact opposite. He was light-skinned, short, slew footed and had a droopy bottom lip. She was loud. He was quiet. She was brash. He was timid. He smoked a pipe. She didn't. She would cuss. He would too. She'd drink a beer on Friday and Saturday nights. He'd drink a bottle of vodka almost every night and then curse some more.

My aunt outweighed my uncle by at least a hundred pounds, maybe more. It was no surprise to see my uncle on any given day or night, stretched out on the front porch or lying on the front lawn, knocked out cold. The reason: more than likely, my aunt had cold-cocked him in the jaw during an argument. My aunt was no longer a spring chicken, but more appropriately, a 58-year-old hen that fought like a full-sized cock.

No matter how many arguments they had or how many knockouts he endured, they truly loved each other. Their marriage stood not only the test of time but also the different challenges that accompanied it. In their forty-six years of marriage, they dealt with the death of their eldest son, the stress of multiple pregnancies by their unwed daughter, the psychological pain of their middle son accidentally losing an eye, my uncle's severe drinking problem, my aunt's epileptic seizures; and more stuff than I care to remember. Nevertheless, through it all, they stayed together and never separated, even once.

By the time my aunt was 60 years old, my grandmother had moved in with them. Once grandmother (a.k.a. The Grand Dame) inhabited the residence, things started coming together. The children of my unwed cousin were no longer allowed to run amok. Now, she and her little ones were assigned regular house chores. Grandmother saw to that. The daily fisticuffs between aunt and uncle diminished and eventually fizzled out. Oh yeah, I had a praying grandmother. And when she wasn't praying, she was pulling rank! On everyone!

At least once during the winter holiday season, either Thanksgiving or Christmas, all of the grandchildren, sisters, brothers, nieces, nephews, uncles, and aunts would meet over at Aunt Willamina's house. We would eat like kings and queens all day and play card games and Pokeno all night. It was wonderful! Grandma breathed new life into Aunt Willamina's home and into Aunt Willamena.

Although she wasn't as spiritual as some of her sisters, my aunt believed in God and wanted to serve him. She became a neighborhood church member, and even though she couldn't really sing, that didn't stop her from joining the choir. Between God, church, grandmother, and her desire, Aunt Willamena transformed into Sister McKay. The woman who would have two beers on Friday and Saturday nights no longer allowed alcohol to enter her home. My uncle understood her screeching halt and accepted the fact that the only vodka he'd be able to sip was either in Russia or at the neighborhood bar.

Even though uncle wasn't very spiritual, he went to church from time to time, if for no other reason than to make my aunt happy. In their forty-sixth year of marriage, my uncle was diagnosed with lung cancer. He died a year later. Though she never publicly shed a tear, on the day of his funeral, my unrefined, loud, overweight aunt sat in the church with head held high and with as much poise and dignity as the queen of England. God helped her to sit regally on the throne and uplift her family.

Some love stories last only a season — some last a lifetime. Uncle Milton died at 70. Aunt Willamena died at 78. Their seasons turned into a lifetime of love and happiness.

Beatrice

Aunt Beatrice was the youngest of my grandmother's seven daughters. She was a change-of-life baby and the last child that my grandmother, then at 55-years-old, would have. Aside from being the youngest, Aunt B was also her mommy's favorite. Grandma made allowances for Aunt Beatrice that her siblings could only dream of.

Aunt B had two children, both boys. Both are grown now with families of their own. And just like her mother before her, Aunt B also has a favorite child; maybe all mothers' do. It's not that she loves him more, but just like her mother, she, too, makes allowances that do not extend past him.

Aunt B was always a good-looking woman who never had problems getting a man; her challenge was keeping one. Thus far, she's been married three times, and not one husband has been the pot-of-gold at the end of the rainbow. In retrospect, husband number one was bad! Two was worse! And three was no lucky charm either! Frankly, if you'd put all three of her husbands in a can – you couldn't get soup!

No one could say that they were terrible individuals, but they were awful for her. It's been told by those who know her best *"that she was no picnic either."* Although she's now in her late sixties, Aunt B is still very attractive and very single. And like most attractive, single, sixty-something-year-olds, Aunt B is hopeful that her marital season will again resurface and soon! Because even though **"hope springs eternal – youth doesn't."**

Aunt B's Husbands:

Jessie

Aunt B married Jessie, her first husband, when she was a twenty-something-year-old fly girl. She looked fly. She dressed fly. She was fly and beautiful. She bore him two sons. Though he loved and adored her, the feelings were not fully reciprocated. Uncle Jesse wasn't the love of her life, but she was the love of his. For them, friendship was a possibility after marriage, but divorce was imminent. Their marriage lasted less than ten years.

Although uncle would drink from time-to-time, his addiction wasn't alcohol. It was love! His blinding love for my aunt made him weak and vulnerable to satisfy every whim and desire that came her way. Because of his inability to say no to her, she viewed him as weak.

In auntie's eyes, Jesse was nothing more than a yes man to be trampled over and disrespected whenever things didn't go her way. For him, this was marital suicide. Their marriage was an endless series of mental slam dunks, which my aunt executed so often, and with such precision, that even basketball legend Michael Jordan had nothing on her.

Throughout their marriage, Uncle could never muster the necessary strength that he needed as a husband. It wasn't until after their divorce that uncle succumbed to his demons and became a drunk. Aunt B walked out of Jesse's life with no intention of ever turning back. Although she effortlessly locked uncle out of her heart, it was hard for him to drink her out of his. Twelve years after the divorce, he was still a yes man, in bondage to Aunt B and the brown liquor he so enjoyed.

After meeting and marrying his second wife, Uncle Jesse started to regain his freedom from the chains that had bound him for so long. It took thirty-five years for him to find, realize, and accept the love of a good woman. He put down the bottle, picked up his manhood, and opened his heart to the relationship that he always wanted and deserved.

Nino

Uncle Nino was her second husband. He was the love of her life; and a triple-negative who partook of drugs, alcohol, and sometimes-other women, but she loved him. She met him when she was thirty-five years old. By age thirty-six, he was incarcerated. By age thirty-seven, they got engaged. Uncle Nino proposed to her during her fourth prison visit with him. She married him during the fifth. They married in the sight of God, the Chaplin, and four other inmates who got married on the same day. Although it wasn't the marriage that dreams are made of or the marital bliss she had hoped for, bi-weekly conjugal visits helped quell her sexual desires until he came home years later.

When Uncle Nino was first released, things were terrific. When his six months in rehab ended, he and Aunt B cohabited as man and wife. He attended every court-ordered counseling session, found a part-time job, and he was drug and alcohol-free. Uncle Nino had become the man of her dreams. He was providing the toe-curling, jaw-dropping, bad-boy love-making that she had dreamt of for so long, and she loved it! Aside from this, he was working steadily. Aunt B was in heaven. But soon, the tide turned, and heaven quickly became hell.

Within months of his total freedom, uncle started acting out. Before long, he returned to his old tricks: not working, selling drugs, getting high, and doing whatever else he desired. Auntie prayed that he would change. Her sisters prayed, and grandmother prayed, but uncle continued on his path of destruction.

Aunt B's winter of discontent with Uncle Nino didn't last very long because God answered someone's prayer. In less than a year, things turned around. And once again, Uncle Nino was drug and alcohol-free, with steady employment working in the laundry. He was washing, pressing, and folding clothes for all of the other inmates on cell-block C. You guessed it; he was back in jail.

Aunt B is proof positive that history can repeat itself. Her first marriage to Uncle Nino happened on the 2nd day, of the 2nd month, during the 2nd year, of his three-year prison stint. As fate would have it, on the 2nd day of the 2nd month, she filed for divorce during the 2nd year of his last incarceration.

Israel (Izzy)

Her marriage to Izzy, husband number three, was doomed from the start. Although he didn't use drugs or drink excessively, he was mean! No... scratch that - he was as-mean-as-mean could be, at least he was to Aunt B.

His meanness gave Aunt B three reality jolts: Jolt 1: She realized that she didn't love him. Jolt 2: For Uncle Izzy, the feeling was mutual. Jolt 3: She should have never married him in the first place. They were married less than one year, but their problems started long before the "I do's" were said. Their problems were two-fold. Uncle Izzy didn't know the Lord, and neither of them really knew each other. They enjoyed the sex, the pot-smoking, the wine, and the laughter, but when the haze cleared and the laughter stopped, there were no binding ties to sustain them. Uncle Izzy liked Aunt B's surface, and she, his, but that was it. When they delved more intimately into each other, neither liked what they saw.

Aunt B was a God-fearing woman who loved and believed in the Lord wholeheartedly. She went to church, studied the Bible, and by all intents-and-purposes, she was a good person, but she wasn't delivered. Even in her fifties, Aunt B still struggled with the negatives that enfeebled her first two marriages: selfishness, attitude, manipulations, and the occasional opiate or ganja haze. Through it all, Aunt B, like her sisters, had a praying mother who stayed on her knees before the Lord, even when her daughters didn't.

It would be easy to say that my aunt got who and what she deserved when she married Izzy because they both shared the same middle name of 'selfish,' but the Bible says, "Judge ye not."

Uncle Izzy left one evening for a pack of cigarettes and never returned. Auntie put out an APB with the local authorities and sought him for three days, calling family, friends, his job, even his ex-wife, but to no avail.

A week later, she received a call. *Was he dead?* Of course, not; unless you consider Delaware, the new-resting home of the dearly departed. When Uncle couldn't take her any longer, he left. And since they slept in separate bedrooms, uncle was able to plot his great escape. He gathered his few belongings bit-by-bit and piece-by-piece until they, and he, were gone. Uncle's move was quiet, subtle, and calculated. Auntie never knew what hit her. Was she hurt? Yes, she was. But since happily-ever-after was never in their future, she took his departure better than expected.

The passage of time can heal most wounds, but it didn't heal theirs. They were far too deep. After nine months of separation, they attempted to reconcile once or twice, but nothing happened. They fizzled-out like an Alka-Seltzer before ever reaching the top.

Ten years have passed since the Izzy chapter of Aunt B's life. She has since moved onward and upward. Though she's still single, she has grown spiritually and emotionally. She is currently *waiting for the man - who is looking for the woman - who is waiting for him.*

Glynnis

Aunt Glynnis is the middle daughter, who is now in her seventies. Aunt Glynnis is still many things: kind, beautiful, feisty, stubborn, God-fearing, loving, creative, intelligent, clever, and sometimes edgy, and not necessarily in that order. But like it or not, that's Aunt Glynnis. And she is - who she is.

I never knew much about her first husband, but her second husband was a character. Not only was he a high-flying, poker-playing, loan sharking, womanizing gambler from the South, but he was tall, handsome, and he could cook. It didn't take long to realize that Uncle Lonzo was a person accustomed to getting his way. But so was Aunt Glynnis. And whenever she wouldn't succumb to his way of thinking, he'd try to out-slick her in some-way-or-another, but he never could. In many ways, "they were two peas from the same pod," except he was the seedling and she the Pisum.

According to my aunt, they met in the late eighties, married in the early nineties, stayed married for five years, and remained separated for fifteen years. But they never divorced. If you think about it, their relationship lasted a long time…but in reverse. Though their marriage didn't endure the test of time, they shared a love and mutual respect that lasted a lifetime.

From day one, they had a marriage that wouldn't rise, no matter what they did. Neither she nor he could set aside adversities long enough to enjoy marital bliss. From time-to-time, Uncle Lonzo would come to my aunt with some type of head game, determined to show her that he was the man. And though his antics worked for a minute, she played head-games too. And hers were way better - with effects lasting way longer. Like I said, Aunt Glynnis is a clever one.

Though total opposites who had very little in common, my aunt and uncle shared one real passion… Poker! They both enjoyed the game and played it well. My aunt, like several of her sisters, loved to gamble. I never said my aunts were perfect. But they were, and some still are, funny, loving, entertaining, kind, and hilarious women. My aunts are known to possess many qualities - some good, some not so good - and though perfection wasn't one of them, good-gambling was.

My aunt and uncle never had children together, but he always stepped-to-the-plate in helping to raise her children, and for that, she loved him, but for that, she didn't need him. Aunt Glynnis played no games when it came to her children. Disrespect was unheard of in her household, and if you veered from the path, hits, slaps, and punishments would abound aplenty.

My aunt had four daughters and two sons from her first marriage. Though she struggled as a single parent, she was determined not to fail. She raised her children to become well-rounded, independent young men and women who were reared to fear three things: The first was God. The second was unmarried pregnancies. The third was HER. Although my aunt was not saved in the eighties or nineties, she believed in God. She made sure that her children went to church and learned about God. So did my grandmother. She was a significant part of all of our lives.

Aunt Glynnis wasn't a churchgoer, but she saw to it her children went to church every Sunday, or at the very least, that they spent Sundays at Grandma's, singing gospel, listening to sermons, reading scripture, and having Sunday brunch.

As one year turned into two and two turned into five, Aunt Glynnis and Uncle Lonzo got divorced, not because they didn't love each other, but because his gambling was at an all-time high and out of control. When Auntie couldn't take it anymore and because her children were grown, she packed up her poker chips and cashed in. But neither she nor grandmother ever stopped praying for Uncle Lonzo. Maybe that's why he never wanted to break free.

Auntie's relationship with Uncle Lonzo was strange to outsiders looking in, but it was normal_to them. For years during their separation, uncle dated a bevy of women. But none could replace Aunt Glynnis. Every holiday would find him dining with Aunt Glynnis and her family, and every special occasion would include an invitation for him to attend. And he would never disappoint.

They stayed separated for fifteen years, and neither ever remarried. Although Auntie had several male friends, she never seriously dated because her husband was still alive. She truly believed in till death, do you part. Separation didn't count.

Yes, Uncle Lonzo was a Southern man; he was loud; he was corny, could cook, and could play some cards. And he loved Aunt Glynnis. Though he wasn't the best husband or her, the best wife, their love and friendship lasted a lifetime.

When the uncle died, he left everything to Aunt Glynnis, money, houses, everything - including his Saturday night poker chips. According to her, at present, he has the best hand.

Lillian

Aunt Lillian was a Renaissance woman in every sense of the word. She could breathe new life into everything. That is everything except her crumbling marriage. Aunt Lilly's eight-year marriage was headed towards collapse, and she never saw it coming. Aunt Lilly loved her husband, and he loved her back. But their love wasn't enough to stop the head-on collision that came their way. Some birds can't fly together for the whole journey - only part of the way.

She met Leon at a New Year's Eve party in the late 1970s. She was thirty-two, and he, a bit older. Aunt Lilly was hard to miss, with beautiful brown skin, long legs, a healthy figure, and loads of style. That was her nickname, "Lilly Style," because she had so much of it. She knew it. You knew it. And everyone else knew it, but it never went to her head. She was giving, down to earth, funny and fun. The only thing that rivaled Aunt Lilly's generosity was her grace and hospitality.

According to Aunt Lilly, Uncle Leon was an eye-catcher too. A dapper gentleman with good looks and a handsome smile, he was hard to miss. They noticed each other from across the room immediately. In her words, "he looked like a bandbox." Translation: He looked good.

Women were always after Uncle Leon, but he paid them no mind. He only had eyes for one woman. And Lilly was her name. Once he met Aunt Lilly, the others became no more than a vapor-Poof!

Within a year, they were married and living the good life. A year after that, they had their first son and only child. Neither of them wanted many children because their lifestyle was so free and unrestricted. After all, there were vacations to enjoy, dinners-out to be had, shopping to be done, and theater shows to attend. Besides that, they had businesses to run. Aunt Lilly had a small clothing boutique, and uncle owned a thriving barbershop. In their world, a house full of chil'lin didn't fit into the scheme of things.

One day, grandmother called Aunt Lilly and said two words, "*Watch him.*"

Naturally, my aunt questioned her with, "*watch who, mother?*"

But she knew grandmother was talking about Uncle Leon, so she didn't persist. My grandmother lived by the belief that if dogs and babies didn't like you, then something was wrong with you, and grandmother's dog, Danger, hated Uncle Leon. Frankly, grandmother wasn't too fond of him either. It's not that uncle had done anything to upset grandmother. Nor had he ever spoke out of line to her, but for some sage and unspoken reason, he just didn't find favor in her eyes.

Even though she had become ill with breast-cancer, Grandma's Sunday dinners never missed a beat. And just like her food, grandma's intuition, wisdom, and sage advice stayed on-track until the day she died. Like I said, "grandma was a praying woman."

Eight-years into their marriage and four years after her mother's death, Aunt Lilly started watching Uncle Leon. Although she couldn't put her finger on it, there was something out-of-place, something slightly askew. It was now time for her intuition to start working. Even though they were married and sleeping together every night, the relationship felt stifled. In the words of Aunt Lilly, "If it wasn't growing, rising, or moving forward - it was stagnant." She once said, "Their marriage didn't have enough yeast."

Uncle Leon wasn't a drunkard or a user of drugs. He wasn't a gambler, and he didn't believe in hitting women. To his benefit, he was a very courteous and well-mannered, stand-up kind of guy who knew how to entertain. On any given day-or-night, and without hesitation, he could drink you under the table without batting an eye or getting drunk. He was a real man's-man. Uncle Leon was strong, friendly, and fun.

He was well versed in sports, politics, current events, history, and a whole bunch of other stuff. Add to this his charm and sex appeal, and you have a retired ladies' man on your hands. Together, he and Aunt Lilly were quite the couple. He didn't run around and brought his money home every Friday night, just like clockwork. But there was something about him that was slowly manifesting. And if it wasn't right, Aunt Lilly was prepared to shut it down!.

One evening Aunt Lilly went to the barbershop to take Uncle Leon to dinner. He was her man, and she didn't need a particular reason to treat him like a king. The lights were on, but there were no customers in the barber chairs, nor were the barbers congregating around the 62" TV, talking trash like usual. Aunt Lilly knocked on the locked door, but no one answered. She used her key, opened the door, and called out to her man - still, no answer.

As she walked into the back office – Aunt Lilly's mouth flew open from shock. Her eyes widened in horror as she saw her king sitting on the desk with his pants down. Her legs went numb when she saw her husband's fully exposed Tootsie Pop being taste-tested by a full-fledged queen. And there was no crown in sight.

As I said, Aunt Lilly was one of a kind. Most women would have probably run out of the room or start swinging. But not her; she just stood there. Deadpan and shocked. When she regained her composure, Aunt Lilly simply turned and walked back from whence she came – never saying a word.

Within 24 hours, at least five different versions of the story had circulated throughout the family. And like boys waiting in line to dance with the prettiest girl at the party, each of Aunt Lilly's sisters called her, one-by-one, to counsel, console, cry, comfort, and at least one, to criticize Aunt Lilly for marrying Uncle Leon in the first place.

When confronted with his act of betrayal, he repeatedly tried to apologize to her, but his "I'm sorrys" and "Please forgive me" fell on deaf ears. Not only did Aunt Lilly stop watching him, but she also stopped talking and living with him altogether. He had become non-existent. He was her version of the invisible man. She didn't see him, wouldn't hear him, and if it weren't for their son, she would have erased all remnants of him.

Aunt Lilly prayed for God to heal her broken heart so that she could show uncle forgiveness. Still, the vision of his odious liaison constantly repeated itself in her mind. She knew that God answered prayers and that it was only Him who could help her to heal, forgive, repair, and move on without Uncle Leon. So, she waited.

Aunt Lilly tried to rid herself of Uncle Leon for almost a year, but he kept resisting. He'd always find some new reason to contest or deny what she desperately wanted - a divorce! Although he continued courting royalty from time-to-time, uncle claimed that what he was experiencing was a phase, not a habit. And he wanted to reconcile with the woman he loved.

Because of uncle's incessant pleading, one day, Aunt Lilly stopped by his house. Nine months had passed, and she was still married to him with no divorce in sight. Reconciling with Uncle Leon wasn't out of the picture if he would change his appetite, maintain faithfulness, and get counseling. After all, he was still her husband.

Though Aunt Lilly carried forgiveness in her heart, she also carried a gun in her purse. Who knows what snapped in her mind when Uncle Leon's door opened. Maybe it was the sight of his half-naked lover or the fact that Uncle wasn't being honest and fooling her again. Whatever the reason, it didn't matter. That day, Aunt Lilly pulled out her gun and shot the king and his queen. Fortunately for her, no one died, but she still went to jail for attempted murder. But God and the judge were merciful, and her jail-time was considerably less than it could have been.

It was during her stint in jail that Uncle Leon and Aunt Lilly found God together. It was because of God's mercy that the judge was lenient in Aunt Lilly's sentencing, and she didn't spend the rest of her life in jail. During her years of incarceration, Aunt Lilly solidified her relationship with God and her husband. On the day of her release, Uncle Leon was waiting for her with his heart-in-hand. He had forgiven her; she had forgiven him; God had forgiven them both.

Just recently, Aunt Lilly and Uncle Leon celebrated twenty-five years of marriage and love, forgiveness and faithfulness, patience and endurance, hope, and happiness. But most of all, they celebrated God for allowing them a second chance to experience His love and the love of each other.

Yes. Grandmother had seven daughters; with seven different styles… Seven different attitudes… Seven different ways of dealing with adversity, and they had seven different ways of preparing food. They all could cook. They all were married. They all prayed. And at different times in their life, they all loved and served the Lord. It wasn't until after Grandmother's death that her daughters figured out what she meant when she would say, "How many cooks are in this kitchen?"

They thought it meant that Grandmother was the Grand Dame in charge. And it did. But aside from that, it meant that the Lord was in the kitchen with her, tenderizing, sweetening, seasoning, and turning her daughters into the women that they should be.

It is because of God's grace and Grandmother's kitchen that the Littleton girls grew into the Littleton ladies who all loved the Lord. And those who remain still love and serve Him well.

CHAPTER 6

Ms. Brown

"Oh, my God. I can't stand that woman," screeched Eben as she entered the house and quickly slammed the door behind her. She threw her purse and computer bag on the floor as if defiant against them and then exhaustedly plopped on the couch.

"Who can't you stand? Queried Linda as she appeared from the kitchen, wiping her hands on her apron and looking at her sister with surprise.

"Ms. Brown. That's who!" snapped Eben.

Linda took a seat beside her. "You mean Ms. Brown, your office manager?"

"NO! I mean Ms. Brown, the one who thinks she's a dictator in a communist regime. Ms. Brown, who acts like a correctional officer at a concentration camp. Ms. Brown, the 9 to 5, night terror who surfaces during the day! You may call her an office manager, but I prefer to call a minion from the pit of ...."

Before Eben could finalize her sentence, Linda interrupted. "No need to continue. I get the message."

She wanted to laugh out loud at Eben's manic posture, but she did not dare. She did, however, turn away for a moment and chuckle inside. Eben was crying out for sisterly advice, and as usual, Linda would heed the call.

"Okay, Eben. Take a deep breath and tell me what happened?"

Eben followed her sister's instructions and started with a deep breath, then added a sip of water and a silent prayer that her internal smoldering would extinguish itself and not return.

"Well," she began, "I had a 1:30 meeting scheduled for today with Ms. Brown."

"About what?"

"About the way that she's always on my back, Linda. She micromanages everyone, but for some reason, she singles me out more. If you need supplies, the supply cabinet is in her office. She doles out ONE no. 2 pencil and ONE ink pen at a time."

Well, at least she's thrifty, Linda thought.

"If you need the key to the restroom, it's on her desk. And if you're running five minutes late from whatever, she's there, looking at you and her watch simultaneously. "I tell you, she's a nightmare!"

"So, what happened at the meeting?" Linda asked impatiently. At this point, she was curiosity's hostage.

"Well…" Eben began. "Ms. Brown did three things: First, she asked me how my parents came up with the name Eben? Because it's such an odd name for a girl.

"Well, it is odd, Eben."

"That's not the point, Linda!"

"I'm sorry. Continue."

"I told her that mom's name was Eve, and dad's name was Benjamin, so they combined the two and came up with Eben. The second thing she did was ask me where I went to undergrad. After that, she quizzed me about my plans for the future."

"And the third thing?" asked Linda.

"After a few minutes of unnecessary conversation, Ms. Brown then got up from behind her desk, opened her appointment book, and said that we have to reschedule because she had a 2 o'clock meeting. She then opened her office door and said that 'we would talk later.'"

"What did you do?"

"Whatta you mean, what did I do? What could I do, Linda, but walk out like a big dummy! Do you know the whole time we were in her office she never smiled once! I tell you that woman is devoid of feelings!"

"Then quit!" Linda said coyly. "You can get a job anywhere. You're only twenty-eight. You're smart. And aside from that, you'll have your MBA in less than a year. So quit!"

Eben threw her a puzzled look, "Why should I quit?" I love working for Dr. Simmons. Why should I let Ms. Brown force me out of my job because she's tyrannical and emotionally shut-down?"

"Well..." Linda continued, "the way I see it - you have three choices..."

"What?"

"One: You can get another job. Two: You can ignore Ms. Brown and act like she doesn't exist, except when necessary, or three, instead of complaining, you can pray and ask God to change the situation."

"What are you talking about, Linda? were Eben's words before standing up. "I do pray about this!"

"Yes. You do pray. I hear you. But you're mostly praying for yourself. God, make her shut up. God, make her leave me alone. It's always about you, Eben. Why don't you try praying for Ms. Brown? God just might listen."

That was Linda's last statement before rerouting back to the kitchen to finish dinner.

Eben sat down and started to rewind the day's events in her mind's eye. After giving it some thought, she came up with *three* ideas of her own on how to handle the *Brown situation*:

The first would be to exterminate Ms. Brown like a giant bug. Second, she would then place her body in an extra, extra-large envelope. Third, she would then ship Ms. Brown's body to one of their global offices with plenty of postage and no return address. PROBLEM SOLVED! And if that didn't work, then she would try prayer again.

Before falling asleep, Eben opened her Bible and read *Psalm 37:4: delight yourself in the Lord, and He will give you the desires of your heart. Commit your way to the LORD; trust in Him, and He will do it....* Eben prayed that God would honor His word and give her the desire of her heart by ridding her of Ms. Brown. Because if he didn't, Ms. Brown's body would probably end up in Tibet with no one to claim it. She smiled at the idea and then drifted off.

It was 6 o'clock when she arose the next morning. 8:38 would find her standing in front of the office elevator, and by 8:43, she'd be at her desk, preparing for her 9 a.m. start time. In her three years of employment, she'd never had unexcused lateness or absence. Though punctuality was essential to her, it was imperative to Ms. Brown, who always arrived between 7:30 and 8:00 a.m.

On any given day, one would find Ms. Brown perched behind her desk like a hen sitting on an egg.

Her appearance was that of an older version of the schoolmarm from the movie *Good Morning Miss Dove*. Aside from punctuality, Ms. Brown was a stickler for many things: a neat appearance, proper grammar, correct information. Moreover, it was essential that you greet her according to the time of day, with either good morning, good afternoon, or good evening, Ms. Brown. "Hi, Ms. Brown" was entirely out of the question.

"Good morning, Ms. Brown," was Eben's greeting before quickly hurrying to her desk. She didn't want to speak, but there was no getting around it. Other than Peggy, the receptionist, Ms. Brown, had a bird's eye view of all who entered.

"Good morning, Eben. Eben..."

"Yes. Ms. Brown."

"Did you see Dr. Simmons downstairs at the cafe? He has a 9:15 meeting, and I haven't heard from him."

"No, Ms. Brown, I didn't see him." Eben hoped that that would be Ms. Brown's only question of the day unless she asked to resume their meeting.

Eben sipped her coffee and waited for her computer's usual five minutes to open its required applications. She smiled as James, her work buddy, appeared from the kitchen sipping coffee and stuffing a cookie into his mouth. The look on his face foretold an impending chinwag.

"Pssst, Eben."

She didn't answer.

"Eben," he said again, "I know you hear me."

"What, James?" she replied with a half-laugh, almost choking on her coffee.

"Did you speak with Ms. Brown yesterday? I had to leave early, and you didn't call me last night with the 411. So, did you talk with her?"

"No," she replied. "I didn't."

"Why? I thought that you were going to tell her how you feel. How we feel."

"I tried, James, but she eschewed me!"

"What?!"

"You heard me; she eschewed me!"

"Speak English, Eben. Whatta you mean, she eschewed you?"

"Just what I said. I went in to speak with her. She asked me fifty million questions about nothing - and then told me that she had a 2:00 meeting. She said that we would talk later. Translation: She eschewed me!"

"Well," he continued, "Are you going back?"

"No. Why don't you or someone else go in and talk with her about office grievances?"

"Because we're afraid of her, Eben."

"C'mon, James. No one here is afraid of Ms. Brown. Maybe no one likes her. But no one is afraid of her."

"Okay, you're right. We're not afraid, but let's face it, Eben. She likes you."

"No, she doesn't." Eben quietly argued.

His reply was a staunch, "Yes, she does."

"Why do you say that?"

"Because," James said with a smirk, "she lets you get two number 2 pencils when the rest of us can only get one."

She smiled to herself; either James was one of the biggest liars who walked the earth, or he was drinking Irish coffee instead of Folgers.

He called out to her again. "Did anyone tell you about Randall and Stephanie in purchasing?"

She started to listen but rebuffed his chitter-chatter by saying, "James, gossip is the devil's phone line. Either you mustn't answer it, or you must quickly hang up. CLICK!" For the first time since she'd known him, James was speechless.

Dr. Simmons breezed by Eben's desk so quickly that she almost didn't see him. Had he not asked her to give him five minutes, she would have thought him an optical illusion. To be a portly man, Dr. Simmons moved with the swiftness of someone half his size. But for him, rushing was par for the course.

"Good morning, Dr. Simmons."

"Good morning, Eben. Take a seat. I'll be with you after this call."

Dr. Simmons lived on the phone. Whenever he was in the office, his whole day consisted of talking to people worldwide. And in at least five different languages. He had one phone, which was strictly for private and personal calls. And another phone with seven extensions. *Thank God for his 'do not disturb' button, or he'd never get a break,* thought Eben. But no matter how many calls he received, every caller felt that they had his undivided attention - because they did. He was a gracious and unbelievably smart CEO.

After five minutes of taking instructional notes to get this, pay that, set up a luncheon here, and book an airline reservation there, Eben was in full swing. She was his "Gal Friday," his go-to-gal to get it done. And she was never a disappointment.

"Eben," Dr. Simmons called out before she exited his office with her pad and number 2 pencil. "Please don't forget the most important thing on your list."

"Yes. I know," she confirmed. Pick up your suits from the cleaners downstairs."

"Thank you, Eben."

"You're welcome, Dr. Simmons."

Dr. Simmons is a man of class, she thought. If for no other reason, he never forgot to say please or thank you.

By 2 p.m., the morning rush was well over, and the p.m. office/client/meeting/and conference-call hoopla was quieting down. James was talking to clients, Jennifer, the payroll coordinator, was confirming work hours, Lisbeth, from housekeeping, was emptying wastebaskets, and the rest of the staff was going about their day. Eben could see Ms. Brown stirring around in her office.

"Eben."

"Yes, Ms. Brown."

"What's the status of the report that I gave you? You know I'll need it back by tomorrow so that I can review it, make changes, give it back, and have it finalized for Thursday's staff meeting."

"I'll have it done, Ms. Brown. I'm just finishing up some things for Dr. Simmons. I'll be on schedule."

Visibly pleased with the information, Eben watched as Ms. Brown went from desk-to-desk gathering information like a little squirrel gathering nuts for the winter.

Eben glanced at the clock, only thirty minutes before quitting time. She would be home by six. By seven, eating dinner, and by eight, she'd be holding the TV remote and preparing to watch her favorite shows.

"Yes," Dr. Simmons."

"Eben, can you stop in to see me before you leave?"

"Yes, sir. I'll be in just before five."

As usual, he was on the phone when she entered his office. She took her regular seat and waited patiently.

"Hi Eben, I know it's late notice, but do you have any plans for this evening?"

She wanted to say 'yes' but answered honestly instead, "No, sir, I'm free."

"Well," he continued, "I'm preaching at a local church this evening, and I'd really like it if you could come out and support me. I'd like to have more than just one person there."

"Hmmm," she thought, church vs. TV. She wished that she had heard the request before committing herself. But she hadn't - so she would.

"Fine, Dr. Simmons. What time?"

He looked at his calendar. "Service starts at 8:00, but they will be serving dinner from 6:00 to 7:45. And the food is good, Eben."

"Okay," she replied. "I'll see you this evening." As she exited his office, Ms. Brown was entering.

"Goodnight, Eben."

"Goodnight, Ms. Brown."

"Oh, Eben," Ms. Brown continued, "will I see you this evening?"

"See me where Ms. Brown?"

"Are you coming to see Dr. Simmons preach?"

The question not only took her by surprise, but it felt like an unpadded punch to the solar plexus. She wanted to scream but somehow feigned a weak "yes" as she shut the door behind her.

One question followed Eben the entire ride home, "Why, Dr. Simmons? Why?"

The church was abuzz with lots of people, music, and singing when Eben arrived. A smiling usher met her at the door and escorted her to her seat. *Nice crowd for a Wednesday night,* she thought. But like herself, she figured that many of them wanted to be spiritually uplifted as well, even on a Wednesday night. She scanned the crowd's faces looking for, but not really wanting to see, Ms. Brown. *Many she won't come,* she thought. TO LATE! As she turned back, she could see Ms. Brown scooting into the pew from the other side.

"Good evening, Eben."

"Good evening, Ms. Brown."

"It's nice to see you here, Eben. Have you ever heard Dr. Simmons preach?"

"No, Ms. Brown, this will be my first time."

"I'm sure that you'll enjoy it."

With that, Eben smiled, closed her eyes, and enjoyed the spirit-lifting gospel music. She needed it.

Her eyes opened when she heard the introduction of Reverend Dr. Howard Simmons. Wow, she thought. Dr. Simmons was a respected leader and dynamo in business economics, but a spiritual leader as well.

Eben listened attentively as her boss spoke of love, compassion, and forgiveness. His sermon was powerful. And in Dr. Simmons fashion, he ended it with six thought-provoking and convicting words, 'Judge not - lest ye be judged.' Immediately Eben thought of her relationship with Ms. Brown.

Just before his address ended, Dr. Simmons offered to pray for those who were sick. He then said that he'd like to pray for someone special who had cancer. Eben looked over at Ms. Brown. She was crying. Eben wanted to give her a consoling hug but thought better of it. She didn't know if Ms. Brown was ready for that kind of emotion.

As many made their way to the altar for prayer, Eben noticed that Ms. Brown was inching up slowly with them. Eben felt convicted about the feelings that she held against Ms. Brown for so long. Linda was right; instead of feelings of disdain, she should have been praying for her.

When Service was over, she congratulated Dr. Simmons on his spiritually uplifting sermon. She started to leave but knowing that Ms. Brown's car was being repaired, she offered her a ride home, hoping that she would say no. But to her surprise, she accepted. *OMG!* she thought, *me and my big mouth!*

After ten minutes of a thirty-minute ride and polite conversation, the ride grew quiet. Eben wanted to talk more, but where to begin? Finally, Ms. Brown slowly opened up. She spoke of her grown son who recently married, her deceased husband, how she still lived in the house they had shared, and that she received her MBA from Wharton just last year. Even though Ms. Brown had accomplished much, Eben could tell from her conversation that she was a lonely woman with not many, if any, friends to speak of.

Eben arrived at work the next morning with a new frame of mind. Today Ms. Brown would see a new Eben, one who was willing to go the extra mile for her, one who wouldn't be so oppositional. Today was going to be a great day! She could feel it.

To her surprise, there was no Ms. Brown. Her seat was empty, and the office dark. This was the first time in almost three years that Ms. Brown wasn't there when she arrived.

Moments later, James arrived with a Starbuck's Mocha cappuccino latte and a hot cinnamon bun for her. Upon receiving these gifts, she almost fainted. Everyone knew that James was a cheapskate. Not selfish, mind you - just cheap!

"You, springing for breakfast," she said, "What's the occasion?"

"Nothing special," Then he burst into a fantastic smile and said, "Just me getting accepted into graduate school - is all!" he almost screamed.

"I'm so happy for you, James," said Eben as she jumped up and hugged him. Which one?"

"Drexel and Temple. I'll have to decide."

"Well, if graduate school acceptance makes you bring in tasties like this, you should get accepted into graduate school more often."

"By the way," Eben asked, "did Ms. Brown have a meeting this morning?"

"Who knows," he replied in usual James fashion. He started to say something else, but duty called, and he answered.

It was just before noon when Dr. Simmons came rushing by with Ms. Brown in tow. For the first time - in a long time, Eben saw her smile. "Good afternoon, Ms. Brown."

"You're a little early, with the time, Eben. It's not quite noon yet, but I appreciate the greeting."

Eben smiled to herself. Ms. Brown was indeed one of a kind.

"Eben..."

"Yes, Dr. Simmons."

"Can you meet with me today at the close of business? I'd like to speak with you after work.

"Yes," she replied, "I will be in at five."

"And don't worry," he said, "You can charge it as overtime."

At five sharp, she entered his office. And as usual, he was on a call. She took her regular seat and waited patiently.

He was about to start when Ms. Brown entered. OMG, Eben thought to herself. They're going to fire me! I'm going to lose my job. Why else would Ms. Brown be here? She silently burdened herself with a million questions. *How will I pay my car note? How will I help Linda with the mortgage? What about my credit cards? Oh God,* she queried. *Why am I losing my job?* In less than a minute, fifty different scenarios played out in her mind.

She was envisioning herself standing in the unemployment line when she heard Ms. Brown's voice. Whew!

"Eben," Ms. Brown began, "Do you think that I'm hard on you?

"Is this a trick question, Ms. Brown?"

"Don't be impertinent, Eben."

"Well, a little, Ms. Brown."

And you're right, Eben. I'm that way because you have lots of potential. You're smart, a quick thinker, people like you, and you think ahead. But sometimes, you let your emotions get the best of you.

Although she heard what Ms. Brown was saying, the only thing that she could think of was getting fired! She wanted to use James' line and tell Ms. Brown to speak English, but she thought better of it. Instead, she asked, "What are you saying, Ms. Brown?"

"I'm saying that the head of a division needs to have a level head at all times, Eben."

"I understand what you're saying, Ms. Brown, but I'm not the head of a division."

"Well," Ms. Brown continued, "that's why we're here."

"What do you mean?" asked Eben.

"Do you remember last night at church when Dr. Simmons prayed for someone with cancer?

"Yes."

"Well, that someone was me. I have stage 4 cancer and less than a year to live."

Eben looked over at Dr. Simmons. He nodded, yes.

"And," Ms. Brown continued, "If you're willing, we would like you to take over my position."

Again, Eben looked at Dr. Simmons. Again, he nodded yes.

"And finally," Ms. Brown continued, "Dr. Simmons is not just my employer, he's also my uncle."

Eben's head wobbled in astonishment. She felt as if she was in an alternate universe? Ms. Brown's cancer, a job offer, Dr. Simmons and her relatives - it was too much information for her to process at once. She stood up and walked towards the window.

Finally, Dr. Simmons had something to say, "I know it's a lot to drop on you at once, Eben, and we're not expecting an answer today. Ms. Brown and I have talked about this for about a month before presenting the idea to you. You're a strong employee, Eben. You'll do a fantastic job as a division head. We both have every confidence in you."

Eben cried the entire ride home. Had God negatively answered her prayers? Had her prayers had anything to do with what Ms. Brown was experiencing? She didn't know. But what she did know was that she felt terrible.

After a ten-minute call to her, Linda was ready with a listening ear when Eben arrived.

"Oh, no!" said Linda. "She has what? She has how long to live?"

Like Eben, Linda couldn't believe what she was hearing, either. When Eben told her about the Simmons/Brown game plan, Linda threw up her hands in disbelief."

Oh my goodness, Eben. Isn't this the woman that you said hated you? The one you said was devoid of emotion. The one you called a…"

Before Linda could finish, Eben interrupted with, "I know. Maybe I was wrong. Perhaps you were right all along, Linda."

That night, Eben prayed like never before. She prayed for comfort and healing for Ms. Brown. She prayed that she would be the best Division manager that Dr. Simmons could ask for.

Over the next six months, Eben and Ms. Brown worked side-by-side during the day; and spent numerous hours together outside of work, becoming friends. Ms. Brown had no daughter, and Eben had no mother. They were a perfect match. Eben even confessed about her plan to ship Ms. Brown to Tibet.

"Oh," Ms. Brown said one day, "you were going to ship me to the Roof of the World, were you?"

"What's the roof of the world?"

"Why, Tibet is, Eben. Didn't you know that?'

"No, I didn't, Ms. Brown. Why do they call it that - and how come you know the answer?"

"They call Tibet the 'roof of the world' because it's about three miles above sea level. Aside from that, some of the world's tallest mountains are surrounded by Mt. Everest and K2. It's also the highest region on earth.

"How do you know this stuff, Ms. Brown?"

"Well, Eben, my husband was stationed in China for several years. We always planned on going to Tibet together - but we never got the chance. Live your life, Eben." Were her last words before drifting off to sleep.

As Eben grew more vital in performing her duties as division manager, Ms. Brown grew physically weaker in her body until she could no longer come into the office. But just like Eben promised, she never left Ms. Brown out of the office loop.

The week of Ms. Brown's funeral, her son asked Eben to read the story of her life. She was happy to read the life of her manager, mentor, and friend. She was amazed to read that Ms. Brown was so accomplished in many areas. She was not just a division manager, but a concert pianist, a literacy teacher who taught ESL to international students. She also counseled women on dealing with a terminal illness. Wow, Eben thought, I'll never misjudge anyone again.

One afternoon while at work, Eben received a sizable box from the Tibetan office. Enclosed, she found a big Hefty trash bag. A label which was addressed to the Tibetan office with no return address. A can of Raid bug spray. And a letter addressed to her from Ms. Brown, which Nadia, the secretary in the Tibetan office, had transcribed. The message read…

"Dear Eben, after sharing with me your penchant for exterminating people and sending them on Asiatic journeys, I had these items sent to you from our office in Tibet. That way, when that feeling resurfaces, and you're ready to execute your plan, you'll have all that you need at your disposal to provide them a wonderful trip!

My suggestion: Start with James!

Fondly, and with sincere admiration,

Clara Brown"

Eben Smiled.

CHAPTER 7

Whenever You Call

Seven years of cooking. Seven years of adult calisthenics. Seven years of being married and feeling like I belonged to someone. Seven years of faithfulness to one who wouldn't be faithful. Seven years of intermittent heartache and the hope that things would change. They didn't! Seven years of unprovoked disappointment from one that I thought loved me.

My husband's infidelity forced me into a life that I didn't want, need, or expect. I believe that marriage should involve God, a man, and a woman. His belief was different; and involved two, three, or four paramours outside of marriage. God was nowhere in sight. Now at fifty-three years old, I'm suddenly divorced, single, and attempting to date again.

Wow!

Now, more than ever, I find myself asking the question, *is it true that God will come whenever you call?* Because Lord knows, I need him to come and help me out of this dating nightmare!

I'm an intelligent, attractive, vibrant, outgoing, and loving middle-aged woman. I long to remarry and share my life, my love, and my bed with someone. And not just anyone! A husband. But where does one find such a person in these *non-committal* times? Let's face it - just because the marriage is over - it doesn't mean that love is.

As I maneuver through single life, two questions remain constant in my mind, *"How do I handle sexual desire in a new relationship? And achieve intimacy without being sexually intimate?"* These questions would be non-existent if I were still married - but I'm not! That last argument between Danny and me was like a bad dream. And when I awoke, my marriage was over.

"When are you going to stop cheating on me?" I hysterically cried out! "When?"

"I'm not cheating!!" My husband fired back with just the right amount of bravado for his story to seem plausible. It wasn't!

"Stop lying!!" was all I could say before leaving the room and walking into the kitchen. I remember hyperventilating so severely that I felt faint. I could hardly breathe. My runny nose and tear-filled, burning, red eyes had me looking more like a Tasmanian devil than a human being. I was a mess.

I sat at the kitchen table, not wanting to move at all. I was numb. I recall wishing that the tea kettle on the stove could fill itself with water and come to a boil without my assistance. It didn't. I did the next best thing: Got up - and lit the stove.

At some point, I noticed several wet spots on the table. I wondered if they were from my tears or splatters from stirring my tea too hard? I didn't know. I didn't care. It was just an irrational thought. The real question that kept reverberating in her mind was, *why?* Why was my husband of seven years cheating? Had I not been a good wife? A good lover...friend? I didn't know. But what I knew for sure was that I couldn't blame myself for his shortcomings. They were his. And his alone.

How many times had I prayed for him more than praying for myself? How many nights had I stayed up late nursing him back to health after an illness? How many tears had I shed in hopes that his cheating would stop? God!!! I cried out! I should have listened to you and never married him in the first place. God had been talking - but I wasn't listening. You need two halves to make a whole loaf. But at 58 years old, Danny was hardly enough to make a sandwich. That's what happens when you try giving the world to someone who knows **nothing** about *geography or math.*

Now, here I am, emotionally vacillating, because what was familiar to me in marriage - is now a challenging spiritual endeavor. Yes, I'm talking about sex.

For many women in my situation, sex outside of marriage is as common as leaves falling from a tree. Don't misconstrue. I'm not judging because once, I felt the same way. I lived in the moment. But going to church and learning more about God - taught me about Him - and me. I no longer want to sully my relationship with God in hopes of a union with someone that may never come. But try telling that to a middle-aged man who's desirous of a relationship with you. Even though I'm thinking celibacy, he's thinking no way! I look to God - he's looking elsewhere. Like an Alka-Seltzer reaching its peak, the relationship fizzles-out before reaching the top.

Even during casual conversations with Christian men, somehow, the tide turns, and their discussions drift towards sex. If we're discussing world issues...SEX comes into play. Politics...SEX. Relationships...SEX. Marriage...double SEX! And let's not forget the character that I met who had six different hairstyles ALL at ONCE. But that's another story for another time. In the past month, I've met approximately 12-15 men. And without question, if you put all of them into a can - you couldn't get soup!

I have tried several Christian and non-Christian internet dating sites in hopes of meeting my spiritual counterpart. Regrettably, I've encountered the opposite. Their profile read: *"single Christian man looking to meet a wholesome Christian female with good morals."* That's what they said - but it's not what they wanted!

Instead, they expected an exchange of illicit photos, phone sex, or at the very least, a videotape of my naughty bits. Add to this provocative conversation with questions like, how long have you been celibate? Do you plan on staying celibate if you're in a relationship? Do you have a list of bedroom do's and don'ts? Do you like this? Have you done that? Etc., etc., etc. It's overwhelming! And once I give my affirmative NO to their exacerbating questions, what usually follows is their swift departure from the phone and no invitation for a first or second date.

My conversations with these men brought to mind the apostle Timothy's words (2 Timothy 1-7) *"There will be terrible times in the last days. People will be lovers of themselves... without self-control, brutal, not lovers of good, treacherous, rash, conceited, lovers of pleasure rather than lovers of God, having a form of godliness but denying its power."* Timothy also says, *"Have nothing to do with such people. They are the kind who worm their way into the households and captivate vulnerable women who are weighed down with sins and led astray by various passions. Always learning but never able to come to a knowledge of the truth."*

This passage forced me to look at my suitors and question myself. *Was I one of those women of which the Bible spoke? Was I willing to settle for someone who wasn't spiritually compatible just so that I wouldn't be alone?* Granted, I'm no teenager dealing with peer pressure. Nor a young adult experiencing passion for the first time. But instead, a mature, level-headed, responsible Christian woman wanting a real, monogamous, marital, adult relationship.

The struggle between *my spiritual correctness* and *my fleshly desires* is like the feud between the Hatfield's and the McCoy's. And it's challenging for me. Not unattainable. But challenging.

Recently, I told one of my girlfriends that I intend to maintain celibacy. Upon hearing this, she coyly asked...

"What are you saving it for? Marriage?

Her look was that of utter surprise when I responded, "Yes!"

Her next response consisted of four words, "Better You Than Me!"

When it comes to sexual relationships outside of marriage, I find myself spiritually wrestling with God's word. Not because I don't believe it. Not because I don't respect it. Not because I don't want to please Him. I wrestle with it because the thought of losing a *possible* Mister Right can be overpowering, especially if you've been single for a while.

I don't know where I will meet my next spouse (Oh, yeah. I plan to marry again) or my significant other, but somehow, fishing in a sea of men or trolling dating websites doesn't work for me. Listening to their neurosis or weeding out their lies from truth requires too much energy. Although I must say, some are incredibly creative!

So, I often ask myself, should my spiritual values and morals take a back seat because of divorce, middle age, loneliness, desire, or the fear of being alone? Of course not. But let's face it, many times they do.

Whether you're in a new relationship or one with a little history behind it, the question is, *"What does a couple do when struggling with sexual desire and they are not ready to take the marital plunge?"* Whether you're eighteen or fifty-eight, a strong desire is just that - a strong desire!

Even though my first marriage didn't work, I can truthfully say, "I'm not bitter, and I look forward to marrying again. My divorce from Danny opened my eyes to many things, including a mind unencumbered with the "W's" of relationships: *When* -will I meet him? *Will* -it last? *What* -if I spend another seven years with the wrong man? These questions prompted me to revisit Prov. 18:21 "*Death and life are in the power of the tongue and those who love it will eat its fruit.*" I've learned to reject the negative and petition the positive regarding relationships and life. So instead of looking, I'm waiting. I'm waiting on God and believing His word in Prov 18:22, "*He who finds a wife finds what is good and receives favor from the Lord.*" I'm waiting for my husband to find me.

There's an adage that goes, "When you get tired of standing - KNEEL." I spend more time with God in hopes that He will continue to quell (but NOT STOP) my sexual desires until the respective time. I no longer accede to negative thoughts like, "You're too old, or you'll never get married again, or where are you going to find a good man? I now realize that not age, doubt, circumstances, or situations can dictate my life–I won't let it! Keeping my body under submission when it doesn't want to submit isn't easy. It's a daily struggle. But each day, I become more victorious than the day before.

Routinely, I make every attempt to avoid those negatives which come to destroy my peace. When addressing sexual immorality, the "*Should I? Or shouldn't I?*" questions still come to mind. But I'm no longer starting from scratch. I'm starting from experience, and experience has taught me to trust God because HE is the author and finisher of my faith.

Heb 12:2.

I humbly petitioned God to quiet (Not Stop) my sexual desires until the right man came along. One day I asked, "God, when will I feel you in my life? I then heard Him quietly answer, **Whenever You Call**. So I did, and He showed up. And, in time, God answered my prayers and gave me the desires of my heart.

I suppose you're wondering what exactly did God do? Well, guess what, y'all, I'm married now. And I couldn't be happier.

Ooh... and my girlfriend, *Miss Better You Than Me!* Called me after I remarried and asked, "when does God hear and answer your prayers? Cause I need His help."

I laughed internally but said aloud, *"Whenever You Call."*

CHAPTER 8

Conversation Closed

Alex said, "I love you," more times than Linn could remember, but only when they were alone. Linn knew that they were in love, but some people had a problem with expression, and Alex was one of those people. Public displays of hugging and kissing were no problem, but open terms of endearment weren't as easy. Sometimes Alex was hard to figure out.

Every now and then, Alex would accompany Linn to church, but if not, Linn never pressed the issue. Everyone found God in their own time, was Linn's belief. Besides, there were too many other things that they enjoyed doing together, especially when it came to kissing, cuddling, and sharing the passion and fun of young love.

Sometimes the sexual enthusiasm between them was so isotonic that Linn would feel overwhelmed. At times like this, Linn knew that decelerating intimate activities and bringing passion to a grinding halt were the best things to do. To this end, Alex took no pleasure, but maintaining virtue was essential to Linn, no matter how strong the desire.

"What's the big deal? "Alex asked with a hint of irritation, "I love you. You love me. Why do we have to wait until marriage, Linn? Sometimes I feel stupid - especially since most of our friends lost their virginity in either high school or freshman year of college."

It was now Linn's turn to be irritated, "How do you know who lost what - or when they lost it, Alex?"

"Because I do."

"Really?" Linn replied with moderate indignation, "Name two people."

"I'll name more than two: Derrick and Cindy, Vince and Lena, Lonzo, and whatever his new girl's name is. As I said, everyone is doing it! Everyone except us that is."

"Maybe they are," Linn replied. "Maybe they don't have the same spiritual conviction that I do, Alex. My spiritual values mean more to me than just having sex because everyone else is. I know it sounds old fashioned and not words that you'd expect to hear from me, but I want to be married to you. I want it to be special because you're special. How many of them can say that?"

Linn looked at Alex fixedly before asking, "You angry?"

"No, not really," Alex replied. "I'm just tired of waiting. I mean, we've been going together for a year. You know me. Aren't you tired of just kissing?"

"C'mon, Alex. We do more than just kiss. We hug. We touch. We laugh, joke, play, talk, disagree (like now). We do way more than just kiss."

Alex hesitated for a moment before speaking and then continued. "Think of it this way, Linn; you're like this exquisite, shiny, new car parked in my driveway. It's mine, I can touch it and show it off, but I can't open the door because I have no key. Do you follow me?"

"Yes...I follow that you're diminishing our relationship to that of a car? Ooh, I'm sorry. I meant to say, a shiny, new car."

"No, I'm not!" Alex replied in a corrective tone. "But remember, I don't have the Christian values that you have. I'd like to, but right now, I just don't. And marriage - who knows when that will happen?"

"I know how you feel," said Linn with a half-smile. "But look on the bright side. Someday we'll be married. I'll be yours forever, and you'll be able to take a ride whenever you want, but for now, the door stays locked. CONVERSATION CLOSED!"

Conversation closed, thought Alex. That was Linn's response after every argument or disagreement that bore no more discussion. Translation: I don't want to talk about it anymore.

Some days Alex would accept these words as final and not persist with the discussion. Today was one of those days. For now, Alex tabled the topic until the next time it would arise.

"Will you call me later?" she asked as she watched him jump over the railing to his house. They had been next-door neighbors since childhood, and not once had he ever fallen during a jump.

"I will," he replied. He gave her a quick kiss before disappearing out of sight behind closed doors.

She opened the door to her own home and entered the house. Her mom was sitting in the living room, talking on the phone to her sister, Aunt Rose. Aunt Rose was her mother's only sibling, and they were very close.

Her mother had a daily ritual; she would come in from work, put down her purse and bags, call Aunt Rose (or vice versa), and they'd talk for an hour or so before she started dinner. Their conversations were heartfelt and hilarious, especially since her mother considered herself to be the Sage-of-all-Sages. Aunt Rose would provide the content for discussion; family matters, work, gossip, whatever - and her mother would spit out advice or opinions to Aunt Rose like skittles.

Her mother gave a quick wave and continued her conversation. "Look, Rose, I've gotta go. My daughter has just walked in. I'll call you later. Sure. I'll let her know that you said hello. WHAT Rose? You say that Archie did WHAT?... I'll talk to you about that situation when I call back. I have some excellent advice on how to handle that. Yeah. 8:00 is perfect. We'll talk after Jeopardy goes off. Okay. Love you too. Bye."

"Hi Darling," her mother said as she stood from the couch to greet her daughter. "How was school?"

"Okay, I guess."

"Just okay, honey?" Her mother asked as she hugged her daughter. "Don't worry. Pretty soon, it'll be over, and you'll be graduating with your master's degree in hand. Your dad would have been so proud of you. How many people in our family have completed a dual degree program, receiving their master's degree at twenty-three years old? Aside from that, you have some fantastic job offers. And who knows, you may even get engaged by then."

"Whatta mean?" she asked.

'Well…" her mother said coyly, "he's graduating too - and let's face it, the man does love you. You've known him practically all of your life. You two belong together. And according to his mother…"

"Oh, mother," she replied blushingly.

"Whatta you mean, 'Oh mother?' Mrs. Franklin told me that when he came home from school yesterday, he took her food shopping. When she went into the market – he went into the jewelry store."

"Look, mom," she said before breaking out in laughter. "You're bad enough. Now you're in collusion with his mother regarding an impending proposal. You two act like spies, mom."

"I'm not in collusion with anyone. We were only talking. Besides," her mother continued, "I thought that you wanted to get married."

"I do, mom. I love him and all, but right now. I'm dealing with intimacy issues. He and I are like Yin and Yang, hot and cold, sweet and sour all rolled up into one. We're both struggling to find a happy medium - but it's difficult."

"Do you want to talk?" her mother asked.

"No, mom. Not really. It'll all work out.

She followed her mother into the kitchen. "Are you hungry?" her mother asked.

"A little."

"Well, sit down and let me tell you what Aunt Rose told me."

She could take no more of her mother's cloak and dagger conversation. And hearing about Aunt Rose was definitely out of the question. After a quick stop at the fridge, she journeyed upstairs to the inner sanctum of her room, ate her leftover chicken salad, and then took a nap.

When she woke, she rolled over and looked at her boyfriend's picture sitting on her night table. *He's so handsome*, she thought, deep dark eyes, black hair, vibrant, sun-kissed skin. And enough muscles to make any girl swoon - and swoon, they did. At 6'2" and 220 pounds, he was hard to miss.

He was the schools' premier running back, and he was something to see. His teammates had nicknamed him 'the plow' because he would mow down everyone in this pathway, time-and-time again. Even though he majored in International Corporate Law, everyone knew a pro football team would probably draft him. He was just that good, and she was proud to be his girl. He was talented, accomplished, well-liked, and humble.

Although they were neighbors and had attended the same schools for years, neither ever paid attention to the other. She thought back, cataloging their years together. **Grade school**: He pulled her hair and called her ugly almost every time he saw her. **Middle school**: He said little or nothing to her and hoped that she'd do the same. **High school**: She would relentlessly tease him and whisper with her girlfriends whenever he would pass them in the hall. **The first year of college**: Social niceties and admiring glances replaced childish exchanges of the past. Singular walks or rides to school no longer existed; plurality was the new watchword. **Sophomore year**: He was no longer a skinny boy, or she, an underdeveloped girl, but he had become a handsome young man, and she, a beautiful young woman. **Junior year**: Their dating evolved into a sincere and committed relationship. Now, as college seniors, they were in love and spoke of making plans for a future together.

She remembered the day when she first noticed him. The football team and cheerleaders shared the same practice field. She was exercising a tumble, and he, running to catch an out of bounds ball. Their collision landed her flat on her back. Although seven or eight people were standing over her, she only saw him.

"How many fingers am I holding up?" he asked, looking down at her.

"I don't see any fingers, only stars," she replied as she tried sitting up.

He chuckled and helped her slowly to her feet.

"Boy, I feel like a bulldozer hit me. How big are you anyway?" She dazedly asked him.

"Around 220 pounds. Give or take a pound or two."

"Well...," she continued, "you and your 220 pounds need to be more careful!"

"I need to be more careful?" he questioned.

"Yes."

"Excuse me, girly, but you fell on me."

"No," she replied. "You ran into me!"

After five minutes of "yes, you did!" and "no, I didn't!" The debate concluded with a mutual "WHATEVER!"

He gripped her tightly and walked her over to the bleachers. Even after she regained her senses and could fully stand independently, she still wanted to feel his muscular arms around her.

The intensity of his strong embrace made her feel like chocolate, melting in the afternoon sun. *"When did this feeling start?"* she asked herself – but she had no answer.

"Are you sure you're alright?" he asked.

After giving an approving nod assuring that she was okay, he let her loose. She watched as he jogged back to the field with his helmet in one hand and her heart in the other.

That's how it started; a month later, they were dating.

She rose early the next morning and readied herself for class. Today she'd be walking to school alone. Although her boyfriend's phone call to her was vague, he did explain that he had a career meeting.

"A career meeting?" she repeated.

"Yes," he hurriedly answered back. "A career meeting. And I'm running late."

"With whom?" was her next question. "You never mentioned it to me."

"I know. I have some decisions to make."

"Why are you so secretive?" she asked.

"I'm not secretive. I just don't want to share it right now."

Her tone was that of a scolding mother, "You should be wearing a cape and a mask because sometimes you act like Sir Paul Dukes at a masquerade ball."

"You mean the secret agent?"

"Yep. The very one."

He laughed. "Just be patient. I'll see you later this evening. Maybe we can grab a burger or something."

Accepting that he wasn't going to divulge any further information, she agreed to meet later, ended the conversation with "Love you," and hung up.

Graduation was quickly coming upon them, and she had no concrete plans for the future. There were a few jobs on the line, but she wasn't sure if she wanted to leave Philadelphia or continue school for her doctorate. The dean had offered a position as an associate professor in Linguistics, but that meant three or four more years of schooling. Moreover, she wasn't sure if she was up to the task. Decisions, decisions, decisions. She'd have to have a sit-down with her boyfriend, especially since she still was in the dark about his career moves. She looked at her watch. The day was going by quickly. Later they'd meet on the porch. Maybe then a discussion would start.

He was sitting on the porch when her door opened.

"Hey, Alex."

"Hi, Linn."

He smiled and handed her a piece of Juicy Fruit gum. It was her favorite. *He seems to be in a good mood,* she thought. Maybe things went well for him today. She was looking forward to a pleasant evening, and not one marred by their differing view on sex before marriage if things got too heavy.

Even though he tried to hide it, he blushed when he saw her standing there. She was such a beauty - and he loved her.

"So, this is the week of the big party," she said.

"Yeah," he replied. "I wish my mom wouldn't do all of this hullabaloo. I'm graduating - not going to war."

"Well, you know how your mother is. I've seen her coming in with packages all week. She's excited! I mean, you're her only son, and she's proud of you. You know how moms are. Remember, mine isn't much different."

"Do you feel like going for a ride?" he asked while pulling her close for a kiss.

"I'm not sure. I still have a few things to do. I was hoping for a quick bite and some conversation. Besides," she continued, "I don't feel like arguing tonight."

"Arguing!" He repeated.

"Yes. Arguing!"

"About what?" he curiously asked.

"You know," she said with a sigh. "Sex."

"Come on...how often do we argue about that? Sure, we disagree, but not all of the time."

She looked at him. "Well...," she continued, "Is this going to be one of those nights."

"No," he said calmly. "I have a solution. Why don't we just sit out here and chill? I mean...you've got things to do, and I have a lot on my mind."

"Anything you wanna talk about?" she queried, in hopes that he would say yes.

"No. Not really."

She had to ask, "What about your career decision? I mean, you haven't talked to me about it at all. Why not?"

Aside from that, he hadn't mentioned anything about their future together either. She didn't like it.

"Look, babe, some decisions a man must make on his own without outside influences. And even though I love and value your opinion, this is one of those times." He knew that she didn't like the answer - but he gave it anyway. He then remembered the adage, "a man's gotta do, what a man has gotta do." And he was sticking by it.

"So, I'm an outside influence..."

He was unsure if she was asking a question or making a statement. And judging by her body language and the look on her face, he was afraid to ask.

Knowing how angry she was becoming, she felt it better to end the conversation before it became too_heated. "Okay," she said as she turned towards her front door. Let's forget about tonight! After all, I don't want to be a negative influence."

She then remembered an adage as well. "Get Lost!" she said, "Now put that in your paper - if you require news." She then turned around, walked into her house, and slammed the door behind her.

"CONVERSATION CLOSED!" She shouted from behind the door. "Now it's my turn!"

By the eve of his graduation party, they were back to normal. She had lain awake practically all night, imagining her reaction if he did propose. And how to hide her disappointment if he didn't. There had been murmurs all week from both her mother and his that he had a big announcement, but knowing him, it could be anything.

She wondered, was it a secret NFL draft? A job offer which he hadn't shared? A proposal? Was he enlisting in military service? She didn't know what to expect. Sometimes his reluctance to share could be so annoying, and no one could force his hand until his time of choosing. But that's what made him so special. He was his own man. She remembered her last birthday outing with him.

"I'm taking you to lunch tomorrow," he said, "so be ready by 9 a.m."

"Nine?" she repeated. "I thought you said lunch."

"I did."

"Who goes to lunch at 9 a.m.?" she asked, being intrigued and excited at the same time.

"We do!." His voice was firm. "Be ready by 9. Love you. Bye."

He was in the car when she opened her front door at nine sharp. He smiled when he saw her, admiring how pretty she looked.

"Wow!" she said, "this must be some lunch date. You're out before me."

"Well...," he started, "you said you wanted some excellent Cajun/Creole food. So, I'm taking you to get it."

Immediately she thought of Catahoula's. It was one of the best Cajun restaurants in downtown Philadelphia. Although she had lived in Philadelphia most of her life, she had only been to Catahoula's once - and it was magnificent.

"Are we going to Catahoula's?" she asked.

"Nope."

"Well, where then? And why so early?"

"You'll see," he replied with a boyish grin.

Twenty minutes later, they were valet parking at the Philadelphia International Airport. Forty-five minutes after that, they were boarding a plane to New Orleans, Louisiana.

"You've got to be kidding me!" she shrieked. "You're taking me to New Orleans for lunch?"

"Yep. Where better to get some good Cajun food than the French Quarter."

Three and a half hours later, they were sitting in Galatoire's Restaurant on Bourbon Street, dining on Crawfish/Shrimp étouffée and Jambalaya. It was a beautiful day. One he would always remember, and she would never forget.

Her thoughts were disturbed by a knock on her door. "Are you still up?" her mother asked.

"Yeah. I'm just thinking."

"Me too." Her mother said with a smile.

"What are you thinking about, mom?"

Her mother leaned down, hugging her tenderly. "I'm thinking about how proud I am of you. And how wonderful you are. I love you, daughter. Now let me give you some sage advice."

She laughed as she pulled the covers over her head. "Goodnight, Mom. I can't do it with you tonight. I don't have the energy. Call Aunt Rose." Her mother laughed, turned off the light, exited the room, and closed the door behind her.

Although they lived next door to each other, he did what any gentleman would do and rang her doorbell ten minutes before the party started.

"You ready?" He asked as she appeared from behind the door.

"I didn't know that you were escorting me." She said with an uncontrollable smile.

"I can't let my girl walk in alone."

"You're so special," she said as she kissed him on the cheek.

They walked through the crowded room, greeting guests, shaking hands, and sharing smiles. She was happy to be a part of his life and, meeting his family and friends from other states for the first time. It was turning out to be a happy and congratulatory event with exquisite food. *His mother is such a wonderful cook*, she thought.

Two hours later, the party was in full swing. It was then that the man of the hour took center stage. After thank yous all-around to his family, coach, friends, etc., etc., etc. for attending, it was now time for him to speak. She wondered, was he going to do it. Was he going to propose in front of all of these people? Or would tonight reveal his big career decision - the one that made him so tight-lipped? Her heart was pounding as if it was beating out of her chest. She had to calm down. She would calm down.

He started with, "It's no secret that I have an announcement to make."

She gasped.

"Over the past months," he continued. "I've had to consider making several life-altering decisions. One I'm 100% sure of, but my path with the other is unclear. Shortly before graduation, a newly-formed football team offered me an opportunity to play football in Cincinnati. As well, a top law firm in California has picked me for a salaried position, which could lead to a promising career. I have not yet decided on either, but I'm thinking of accepting the NFL opportunity and moving to Cincinnati. I'm sorry that I've been so secretive, but I wanted to weigh both decisions without outside influence."

She couldn't believe what she was hearing. Had her boyfriend already decided his future without considering her, especially when she shared everything with him. At that moment, their eyes locked. Though he said nothing, his eyes spoke a million words—none of which she clearly understood.

She couldn't believe him. She wanted to run out of the party, but it would be too apparent that she was devastated. California! Cincinnati! The words reverberated in her mind. Both were a total surprise to her. She felt blindsided. She asked herself, where was the love that she thought they shared? But more importantly, where was God in this situation. She wanted to cry.

"As I was saying," he continued, "With such life-changing decisions, one has to make the right choice. And for me, none of these choices would be right unless I discussed them first with the woman that I love and want by my side."

It was then that Mr. Lindon Oliver Franklin (lovingly referred to as **Linn**) walked over to his girlfriend, Miss Alexa (**Alex**) Rebecca Cunningham, and got down on bended knee. He opened up the small box to a beautiful 2-carat princess cut diamond ring and presented it to her.

He then took Alex by the hand and said, "Alex, would you please do me the honor of being my wife."

The tears forming in Alex's eyes were no longer tears of sadness but tears of happiness. Alex shrieked with excitement as she said, "Yes."

Linn looked at his wife-to-be and said, "I'm applying for my driving license today, Alex." She hugged him and kissed him passionately. They both smiled.

Three months_before their move to Cincinnati, they were married. On that night, their wedding night, Alex finally understood what Linn meant when he would quote the scripture, *"He who finds a wife finds a good thing and obtains favor from the Lord."*

In her mind's eye, she remembered how pushy she sometimes was when it came to having sex. But no matter how much she argued or how many tantrums she threw, Linn remained steadfast in **his** convictions - and no meant no!

Alex now realized that saying CONVERSATION CLOSED meant more to her husband than just saying no. He was working towards being the man that God wanted him to be – strong, firm, loving, and steadfast. Following the crowd in a sport as pro football could ruin a marriage because a weaker man could easily fall when tempted. But if Linn could remain steadfast by saying "no sex" to the woman he loved because of his relationship with God, she knew that she had no worries. She understood that now, and she was thankful.

As they lay discussing their plans for the future, Linn hugged his wife and whispered in her ear, I've waited a long time for this night, Alex. I wanted to do it God's way.

"Wow!" she said. "I guess you did have a plan."

"Yep," he said. "And guess what?"

"What?" she responded.

"We're married now," said Linn as he clicked off the light. "CONVERSATION CLOSED!"

DOWNLOAD YOUR FREE GIFTS

Read This First

Just to say thanks for buying and reading my book, I would like to give you a 100% bonus gift for FREE, no strings attached!

To Download Now, Visit:
www.AuroraAvendorSpeaks.com/freegift

I appreciate your interest in my book, and I value your feedback as it helps me improve future versions of this book. I would appreciate it if you could leave your invaluable review on Amazon.com with your feedback. Thank you!

www.ingramcontent.com/pod-product-compliance
Lightning Source LLC
Chambersburg PA
CBHW052008240626
47153CB00008B/2793